A madman se
Core and only Dar
It's Carnaval .... Dane
Maddock and the crew of *Sea Foam* aren't in town to party. They're chasing the rumor of an ancient Roman shipwreck in the murky waters of Guanabara Bay, a rumor that, if true, will rewrite the history of the Americas. What they find instead will cast new light on one of the strangest murder mysteries of the 20th century, and thrust Maddock and his friends into the midst of a diabolical plot to destroy the Church.

DESTINATION: RIO is the first in a new series of stand-alone novellas by USA Today bestselling author David Wood and prolific action-adventure novelist Sean Ellis. Each new story in the DESTINATION: ADVENTURE series will transport Dane, Bones and the crew of *Sea Foam* to an exotic and exciting locale, where treasure, mystery, and adventure await!

Praise for David Wood and Sean Ellis!

"Dane and Bones.... Together they're unstoppable. Rip roaring action from start to finish. Wit and humor throughout. Just one question - how soon until the next one? Because I can't wait." -*Graham Brown, author of Shadows of the Midnight Sun*

"What an adventure! A great read that provides lots of action, and thoughtful insight as well, into strange realms that are sometimes best left unexplored." -*Paul Kemprecos, author of Cool Blue Tomb and the NUMA Files*

"Ellis and Wood are a partnership forged in the fires of Hell. Books don't burn hotter than this!" -*Steven Savile, author of the Ogmios thrillers*

DESTINATION: RIO

A DANE MADDOCK ADVENTURE

DAVID WOOD
SEAN ELLIS

Destination: Rio
Copyright 2018 by David Wood

Published by Adrenaline Press
www.adrenaline.press

Adrenaline Press is an imprint of Gryphonwood Press
www.gryphonwoodpress.com

Cover design by Bees' Knees Creatives

This is a work of fiction. All characters are products of
the authors' imaginations or are used fictitiously.

ISBN-13: 978-1-940095-84-4
ISBN-10: 1-940095-84-0

BOOKS and SERIES by DAVID WOOD

The Dane Maddock Adventures
Dourado
Cibola
Quest
Icefall
Buccaneer
Atlantis
Ark
Xibalba
Loch
Solomon Key

Dane and Bones Origins
Freedom
Hell Ship
Splashdown
Dead Ice
Liberty
Electra
Amber
Justice
Treasure of the Dead

Adventures from the Dane Maddock Universe
Destination-Rio
Destination-Luxor
Berserk
The Tomb
Devil's Face
Outpost

Arcanum
Magus
Brainwash
Herald
Maug

Jade Ihara Adventures (with Sean Ellis)
Oracle
Changeling
Exile

Bones Bonebrake Adventures
Primitive
The Book of Bones
Skin and Bones
Venom

Jake Crowley Adventures (with Alan Baxter)
Blood Codex
Anubis Key

Brock Stone Adventures
Arena of Souls
Track of the Beast (forthcoming)

Myrmidon Files (with Sean Ellis)
Destiny
Mystic

Sam Aston Investigations (with Alan Baxter)
Primordial
Overlord

Stand-Alone Novels
Into the Woods (with David S. Wood)
Callsign: Queen (with Jeremy Robinson)
Dark Rite (with Alan Baxter)

David Wood writing as David Debord

The Absent Gods Trilogy
The Silver Serpent
Keeper of the Mists
The Gates of Iron

The Impostor Prince (with Ryan A. Span)
Neptune's Key
The Zombie-Driven Life
You Suck

BOOKS and SERIES by SEAN ELLIS

The Nick Kismet Adventures
The Shroud of Heaven
Into the Black
The Devil You Know (Novella)
Fortune Favors

The Adventures of Dodge Dalton
In the Shadow of Falcon's Wings
At the Outpost of Fate
On the High Road to Oblivion
Against the Fall of Eternal Night (with Kerry Frey)

PROLOGUE

Bruno Alberto Santo paused to light a *cigarro* before approaching the crime scene. As the *Delegato* of the *Polícia Civil do Estado do Rio de Janeiro*, he was seldom called to a crime scene. When it was, it was never good. He took a long, slow drag, letting the acrid smoke burn its way down into his lungs. He held it there for a few seconds, savoring it, before setting the cloud of smoke free into the winter air. His shoulders heaved with mirthless laughter. Winter in Rio de Janeiro was not exactly cold, and temperatures were rising with the approach of spring. Already, sweat beaded on the back of his neck. He took another puff, gave a shake of his head, and made his way toward the circle of uniformed men standing in a patch of tall weeds atop Vintem Hill.

"*Delegato*, thank you for coming." Oscar Torres, a lean man with greasy black hair and a pointed chin, greeted him.

"*Investigador*," Santo replied with a curt nod, "what do we have here?"

"Something strange."

Santo took another deep drag off his cigarro and blew it out his nose. "Is anything truly strange in our line of work?"

"In this instance, the answer is 'yes.'" The *investigador* stepped aside to give Santo a clear view of what lay atop the hill.

Santo took two steps forward and froze. Absently, he

flicked his *cigarro* aside and stood staring at the bizarre scene laid out before him.

Two men, dressed in business suits, lay dead on the ground. Despite the warm, clear day, each wore a raincoat over his suit. But that was not the oddest thing about the scene. Each man also wore a lead mask cut roughly in the shape of sunglasses without the arms.

"A boy came up here to fly his kite, and found them like this," Torres said.

Santo was still gazing at the bizarre lead masks. "Were they expecting radiation?" he asked.

"We will have the area swept for signs of radioactivity, but I can't imagine why they would expect such a thing," Torres said "The raincoats are odd, too." He glanced at the sky.

"Not if they have been lying here for more than a day or so. It has been rainy of late."

Torres nodded.

"Do we know who they are?"

"Manoel Pereira da Cruz and Miguel José Viana. Electronics repairmen from Campos dos Goytacazes,"

Santo frowned. "That is two hundred kilometers away. What were they doing here?"

"We don't know. There's no vehicle nearby and neither had any cash to speak of on his person."

Santo continued to take in the scene. Nearby lay two towels, an empty water bottle, and a notebook.

"What is the notebook? Have you taken a look?"

"I wanted to leave it in place until you had the opportunity to inspect the scene, but I did open it. The first few pages contain a list of electronic parts numbers perhaps pertaining to their business. But the notebook also contains what appears to be a set of instructions."

Torres took out a note pad and flipped through the pages.

"It reads, '*16:30 be at agreed place, 18:30 swallow capsules, after effect protect metals wait for mask signal.*'"

"*Louco,*" Santo whispered. "Did you find any capsules?"

"We did not. Perhaps this is some sort of death cult? Locals claim to have spotted flying saucers in the area. Maybe these men thought that if they swallowed the capsules, they would be taken aboard the spaceship?" Torres lapsed into silence, his cheeks reddening. Perhaps he realized how absurd this sounded.

Santo did not chastise him, but merely nodded. Crazy did not mean it was not true.

"Perhaps, but we follow the evidence, do we not, *investigador*? We don't even know if these capsules exist, much less whether they swallowed them."

Torres nodded. "As you say, *delegato.*"

Santo tried to process the information he had at his disposal. *Be at agreed place* likley meant the two had scheduled a meeting with someone. Was it here, in the middle of a well-to-do suburb, or had the meeting occurred somewhere else, and the bodies dumped atop Vintem Hill to be discovered later? *Swallow capsules, after effect protect metals.* That bit was odd. Were they to be taken as two separate instructions? Were the men protecting metals or was there a missing word that would suggest that swallowing the capsules would convey some form of protection from a metal of some sort? He thought immediately of uranium. Were they perhaps buying or even selling material to make a bomb?

"Wait for mask signal probably means a signal to put

on the lead masks," Torres offered, as if reading his mind. "The wearer would be blind once the masks were donned."

"Blind them then kill them?" Santo said.

"There's no obvious sign of death, although the medical examiner will be better able to tell us."

Santo nodded slowly. It was strange. Damned strange.

"Anything else to tell me?"

"Not at the moment."

"Very well. If you are satisfied that the scene has been thoroughly documented, you may have the bodies removed for examination. Also, I want the area searched with a fine-tooth comb. Don't miss anything."

"These weeds make it difficult, *delegato.*"

"Then today you will be gardeners. Pull them up one by one if you must, but do not miss a crucial piece of evidence. Keep me apprised of all developments and I will let you know if I have any thoughts on the subject."

Torres inclined his head, then turned and began barking orders.

Santo headed back to his car, lighting another *cigarro* to steady his nerves and help focus his thoughts. Torres had been right to call him. This was unlike any case he'd encountered in his career. He knew he had to solve it.

He had almost reached his vehicle when a nearby sound caught his attention.

"*Delegato*, a word?" The speaker stood nearby, half obscured by the evening shadows cast by the nearby trees. He was a hulking figure dressed in an expensive suit.

Santo was immediately on his guard.

"Who are you?" he snapped.

"An ally." The man raised his hand, and for a moment Santo thought the fellow might have a gun, but instead, the newcomer flashed a fat signet ring. Even in the dimming light, Santo recognized the symbol: a circle emanating a series of rays, inside was inscribed a cross, three nails, and the letters IHS. "You are a believer?"

"Of course I am," Santos said.

"God needs your help." The man approached, and Santo appreciated just how massive he was. If he hadn't been a man of faith, Santo would have drawn his weapon, just to be safe. The man leaned in and whispered a name in Santo's ear.

"What..." Santo's mouth was suddenly dry. "What does he want with me?"

"Nothing onerous, I assure you. Just make sure that this crime," he pointed in the direction of the hilltop, "is never solved."

"I'm not sure how I can do that."

"You can. The bizarre nature of the scene guarantees that the public will accept this as a so-called, unsolved mystery. Simply do not press too hard, and make certain that the organs are not examined."

"How could I possibly explain if there is no medical examination?"

The man looked thoughtfully at the purpling sky. "Organs can decompose rapidly in hot weather, can they not?"

Santo understood immediately. "I'll see to it."

The man gave a small bow. "God thanks you for your service."

ONE

For a fleeting instant, all Dane Maddock could see was blue sky. Earlier, he had noticed a few specks in the cloudless azure canopy, gliding shapes that looked like enormous tropical birds. They were not birds but they were living creatures—humans, in fact—soaring across the sky, suspended under brightly-colored crescent-shaped nylon "wings"—paragliding airfoils. But in that moment, there was only pale blue infinity before him. Then, cool water enfolded him, and the flawless turquoise above dissolved into a froth of churning bubbles. He twisted around, reorienting himself so that he was staring down, and began kicking with his flippers to hasten his descent into the depths. He tried hard not to think about what he was actually swimming through.

Almost as soon as he began his descent, the voice of his partner, Uriah "Bones" Bonebrake sounded in his ear. "I feel bad for you, having to swim in all that crap."

Maddock didn't think Bones felt bad at all. He also knew that Bones wasn't using the word "crap" in a figurative sense. The six-and-a-half foot tall Cherokee was incapable of resisting the urge to indulge in "toilet" humor.

Maddock smiled behind his full-face diving mask. "We can always trade places," he retorted, just as disingenuously. The Casio Logosease ultrasound underwater communicator clipped to one of the straps on his face mask transmitted his voice with almost no distortion. He had to admit, there were times he wished something would distort Bones' voice, mostly when his friend was trying to be funny.

As the senior member in their partnership and the owner of *Sea Foam,* the motor yacht from which they operated, Maddock had exercised his executive privilege to make the first dive on the target site, and he wasn't about to relinquish it now. Maddock also preferred to dive alone, which was strictly speaking, a violation of one of SCUBA diving's sacred rules, but he craved the solitude of solo diving, and besides, if he ran into any trouble, the surface was close enough for him to make a free ascent on a single breath. He wouldn't even have to worry about decompression sickness.

"Nah, it's cool. You're already in the water," Bones replied after a moment probably spent weighing the merits of calling Maddock's bluff. "No sense in both of us stinking up the place." He paused. "I think I'll just wait til we get home and take a dive in my septic tank, instead. That's probably cleaner."

Maddock and Bones were treasure hunters specializing in the location and exploration of sunken shipwrecks. They'd first met in the Navy, where they had gone through SEAL training together. Despite a lot of initial friction between them, the two had eventually become fast friends, brothers in almost every sense but the literal. After leaving the Navy, both men had channeled their love of diving and adventure into searching the world, particularly the hidden world beneath the seas, for the treasures of the ancient past.

They weren't in it for the money, which was probably a good thing since gold-laden jackpot discoveries like the *SS Central America* or the *Nuestra Senora de Atocha*, were few and far between. Maddock wasn't chasing gold, though sometimes they got lucky and found it. Often enough to make a living, anyway. Most of the wrecks he and the crew of *Sea Foam* explored were valuable only in a historic sense, but the truth of the matter was that he just loved diving. He was never more at home than when in the water.

But not all water was created equal, and Guanabara Bay, bracketed by four major Brazilian municipalities, was less equal than most. Anyone who watched the news had heard about the issue with the 2016 Olympic games in Rio de Janeiro. The water was highly unsanitary, full of raw sewage. Despite the stunning blue appearance, drinking from the bay was a great way to get deathly sick.

But Maddock knew he would be fine. He had taken all the necessary precautions, including getting a Hepatitis A booster vaccine. His Camaro Arc Tec 2.0 dry suit and Ocean Technology Guardian full-face dive mask enclosed him as effectively as a space suit, though he would have to spray everything down with disinfectants when he got out. Still, the thought of the waste through which he now swam twisted his gut.

And if they found what they were looking for, it would be more than worth whatever actual or perceived risk he was taking.

The object of their current search would, if they actually found it, upend five centuries of accepted history.

According to the textbooks, the European discovery of Brazil had occurred in 1500, when Portuguese explorer Pedro Álvares Cabral made landfall and claimed the territory for the Portuguese Empire. In the late 1970s however, a marine archaeologist exploring the area near Guanabara Bay announced his discovery of several *amphorae*—large earthenware jars used by ancient Greek and Roman mariners to store grain, wine and oil for long voyages—which he believed to be evidence of an early Roman presence in the area. Subsequent investigations however proved controversial, with accusations of impropriety and theft of artifacts, which ultimately culminated in a total ban on underwater exploration in the bay. The archaeologist believed the ban to be motivated by fear of challenging the accepted historical narrative, but whether or not that was true, the search for Roman artifacts in Guanabara Bay had gone fallow and stayed that way for more than thirty years.

Until now.

Although the general ban was still in effect, the Brazilian government, at the urging of the United Nations' Global Heritage Commission, had decided to put the mystery to rest once and for all, and to that end had contracted Maddock and the crew of the *Sea Foam* to conduct an exploratory survey of the site.

Maddock was usually very methodical about his surveys, but a recent development had added new urgency to the search. His Holiness, the Pope had made the unexpected decision to visit his native Buenos Aires for Ash Wednesday, just a few days hence, and would be making a brief stop in Rio De Janeiro to conduct a special service at the city's most noteworthy landmark, the statue of Christ the Redeemer on Corcovado Mountain. With the world spotlight again focusing on Rio de Janeiro, the Brazilian government was hoping to capitalize on the moment with proof of an early Roman presence in the Americas, and it was up to Maddock and his crew to deliver it.

Aside from making the water unsafe for human

consumption, the pollutants also created periodic algae blooms, which depleted the water of oxygen and effectively turned the bay into a dead zone. While this was a tragedy from an environmental standpoint, it had proved to be a blessing in disguise for Maddock's search. The corals which had once covered the bay floor were dead and gone, crumbling away to reveal a veritable graveyard of wrecks, many still mostly intact under the accumulation of silt. Hopefully, one of them would prove to be an ancient Roman merchant vessel.

A few feet below the surface, the water was a murky greenish-yellow, the visibility reduced to mere inches. Beyond that, the sediment formed an impenetrable cloud to block the rays of his head-lamp. Maddock continued to kick his way through it, knowing that the bottom— and the target they had identified in their earlier sonar sweep—was a good forty feet down. The floor of the bay was covered in a uniform layer of rusty-colored silt, and as it came into view, Maddock slowed his descent, flattening out to avoid disturbing it with his flippers. Despite the poor visibility, he easily spotted the irregular protrusion that could only be the remains of a sunken ship. His heart raced.

"Contact," he said. "It's a shipwreck all right."

"Cool, but is it the right one?" Bones replied, his voice sounding a little smaller than it had closer to the surface but still perfectly audible.

"Tell you in a minute or two," Maddock answered.

He swam up and down its length, visually confirming what the sonar profile had indicated. The protrusion had the right shape, but was about sixty feet in length, which was actually quite small for a sea-going vessel. Maddock's boat, *Sea Foam* was an eighty-footer.

Roman triremes were often twice that long, but when it came to seaworthiness, size wasn't everything. The *Santa Maria,* largest of Christopher Columbus' exploration fleet, had been only about sixty-five feet in length. Maddock didn't doubt that they had found a shipwreck, but proving—or disproving—that it was of ancient origin would require specific proof, which meant getting a lot closer.

He made another quick circuit, scanning for smaller protuberances in and around the outline of the wreck that might indicate artifacts, perhaps even some of the amphorae which had initially prompted the search. Midway down the length of the wreck, something caught his eye and he moved closer to investigate.

Covered by silt, he could only approximate its shape, but its outline—about three feet long and perfectly straight—was unusual, and certainly not something naturally occurring. He gently fanned the silt away, creating a small cloud around the object which quickly cleared to reveal what looked at first glance like a piece of corroded old pipe. Maddock gently took hold of it, and then with painstaking slowness, began to lift it free of the muck.

"Looks like I've got something here."

"Yeah?" Bones replied. "Is it something Roman?"

The artifact came free in his hands, shedding mud and silt in another small cloud. When it cleared, Maddock saw that the object was not as perfectly symmetrical as it had appeared, but had irregularities along its surface. Some of these served as braces that had once connected the pipe to something—a piece of wood, Maddock guessed, though there was nothing left of that now. Despite the ravages of time and oxidation,

Maddock immediately recognized what it was.

"No," he said with a sigh, making no effort to conceal his disappointment. "It's a gun barrel. Colonial era. A musket or maybe an arquebus."

"Maybe a Spanish soldier dropped it overboard," Bones suggested, though he didn't sound hopeful. "And it just happened to land right on top of the Roman ship."

"Portuguese," corrected another voice on the communications line. It was Corey Dean, the crew's resident tech expert.

"Same difference," Bones shot back, dismissively.

"Or French," Corey continued. "The Huguenots built the first settlement in Rio."

"Screw the French," Bones muttered. Maddock ignored him.

"Could be," Maddock replied to Corey, though he too thought it was an unlikely scenario. The simpler explanation was that the wreck was from the Colonial period—Sixteenth or early Seventeenth Century. Still, a wreck was a wreck, and one never knew what might turn up. "I'll keep poking around. See if I can find anything else."

He moved away from the still-settling silt cloud, and resumed his meticulous scan. After a few seconds of this, he spotted a pyramid-shaped bump in the silt.

He fanned his hand over the protrusion, stirring up another small but manageable cloud of sediment, but through it, he could distinctly see something glittering in the diffuse rays of his dive light.

"What's this?"

"What have you got?" asked Corey, eagerly.

"Tell you in a second," Maddock replied. "It's metallic, whatever it is."

"Maddock, if you've found a freaking hubcap…" Bones warned.

Maddock extended a gloved hand forward, cautiously probing the spot, and immediately felt a solid surface under his fingers. The pyramid had three faces rather than four and its edges continued down into the thicker sediment layer, and was buried deeply enough that hecouldn't shift it. Maddock immediately realized his mistake; it wasn't a pyramid, it was a corner. "I think it's a chest of some kind."

There was silence on the line for a moment, and then Corey let out an exultant whoop. "Yes! Pirate booty beats Roman wine jugs any day of the week."

"I'm more of a jugs man than a booty man myself," Bones chimed in.

Maddock grinned behind his mask, not at Bones' quip but at Corey's excitement. While he doubted they would find a chest overflowing with doubloons and emeralds, it wasn't completely beyond the realm of possibility. Rio had seen its share of adventurous pirates and privateers. In 1710, an entire fleet of French privateers had been defeated trying to take the city, and just a year later, Rene Duguay-Trouin succeeded, filling seventeen galleons with loot. Two of those ships had been reported lost, whereabouts unknown.

"Let's not go spending it until we actually have it in our hands," Maddock cautioned, brushing away more sediment.

"Slow your roll, Maddock. I'm coming down," Bones declared. "Give me a minute."

Maddock had no intention of killing time while his partner suited up and made the descent. He moved closer to the find, fanning away the cloud for a better look at his discovery. Once again, his light was reflected back by a metallic surface—a golden metallic surface. The object did indeed appear to be a chest, roughly rectangular. It had come to rest at an angle, so that one corner was jutting up from the surrounding sediment. The lack of corrosion on the metal panels seemed to confirm that the metal was gold, which struck Maddock as somewhat unusual since most chests were made of wood or leather, and only banded with metal to provide additional structural strength.

He brushed away more silt, trying to get a better sense of the chest's dimensions, and in so doing, exposed a large sculpture affixed to one of the panels. His first thought was that it was a bas relief—a decorative embellishment, but as the accumulated muck slid away, so did the carving. When he tried to pick it up, he discovered that despite being smaller than a dinner plate, it was unusually heavy—easily fifteen pounds.

Heavy like gold.

He lifted the object into the beam of his light, and felt his pulse quicken.

It *was* gold.

The object appeared to be a decorative headdress or perhaps a crown. It had been fashioned to resemble a crest of feathers, each of which had been accented with bright blue cloisonné. The delicately carved feathers were arrayed around a bowl-shape which looked just big enough to rest on a man's head. Part of the bowl was slightly misshapen, pinched forward just a little, jutting out like a nose from a face. It took Maddock another moment to realize that the deformation was deliberate.

"It's a mask," he realized aloud.

"What was that? Is something wrong with your

mask, Maddock?" Corey asked.

"No. I found a mask. A decorative golden mask."

"Did I hear 'golden'?" Bones chimed in.

Maddock grinned. "Looks that way. Kind of reminds me of a native headdress with tropical feathers. No eyeholes though."

He brought the artifact closer to his face, imagining how it might have been originally worn, but as he did, he glimpsed something moving in the reflective inner surface of the mask.

It's just Bones, he thought, and started to turn. "That was fast—"

Then something slammed into the side of his head and cold, foul water flooded into his eyes, nose and mouth.

TWO

Maddock's SEAL training instantly kicked in. Instead of gasping in surprise—and drowning—he clamped his mouth shut, threw his hands up to ward off any follow-up attacks, and twisted away from the unseen attacker. The heavy golden artifact fell from his grasp, his attention now focused on finding and recovering his SCUBA mask.

He found it almost immediately, still attached to his regulator hose, the dive-light clipped to the head straps shining uselessly downward. He kept his eyes open, despite the risk of exposure to the contaminants in the water, but he might as well not have bothered. The attack and his subsequent response had stirred up a massive cloud of silt which, combined with the blurriness of the water, reduced his visibility to almost zero.

There was no sign of his assailant but he remained wary, turning constantly so that the next assault, if it came, would not take him completely by surprise, even as he cleared the mask and pressed it to his face. He blew out the breath he had been holding, used it to expel most of the water trapped inside the full-face breathing apparatus, and then drew a cautious but much needed inhalation.

"Bones," he gasped. "There's someone down here."

He didn't hear a reply, and didn't wait for one. In all likelihood, the Logosease transmitter had been knocked loose during the attack and his message had gone unheard. He had to assume that any help would be a few minutes in coming, and that was a few minutes he didn't have. Restoring his air supply had been his first priority, and with that done, he was ready to move on to the next. Still holding the SCUBA mask in place with one hand, he kicked away from the silt cloud, playing his light in every direction, searching for his attacker.

It was a wasted effort. Visibility was still limited to just a few feet. He could only tell which direction was up by following his bubbles.

Then it occurred to him that his attacker would be having the same problem.

He switched off his light and was instantly plunged into darkness.

But not quite total darkness. Off to his left, he could just make out faint illumination—an artificial light source—moving away from his location. He took a second to secure the mask straps in place, and then struck out in the direction of the glow, swimming furiously. The light grew brighter with his approach, resolving into two figures in SCUBA gear. The men weren't swimming so much as shuffling across the sea floor on their flippers, a long plume of disturbed sediment trailing out behind them. The reason for this odd form of travel became apparent a moment later. The men were carrying small but weighty burdens. One had the golden mask, the other held a metallic cube about twelve inches on each side—the chest that had first attracted Maddock's attention.

Up to this point, Maddock had not allowed himself to speculate on the identity or motive of the attackers, though with this discovery, he could hazard a guess. The men were almost certainly rival treasure hunters, shadowing him in anticipation of just such a discovery.

It wasn't unheard of for unscrupulous relic seekers

to spy on the competition, pillaging a site after the legitimate claim holder did the hard part of pinpointing a wreck. Evidently the golden artifacts had been too tempting to pass up, prompting them to risk underwater piracy, but their prize was now an anchor, hampering their escape. The men had to be operating from a nearby dive boat, though Maddock could not recall any other vessels in the area and knew that the crew of the *Sea Foam* would have alerted him to any activity. He could not imagine how they had been able to approach unnoticed, to say nothing of finding him in the murky depths, but clearly they had not given much thought to their getaway plan.

Or maybe they had.

As he arrowed through the water toward them, legs driving him forward with powerful kicks, Maddock noticed a barely visible thread of monofilament attached to the belt of the nearest diver—the one carrying the chest. It was a lead line, snaking out into the darkness, though where it was leading became apparent a moment later when the divers' lights revealed something resting on the bottom, just a few yards ahead. The object resembled a pontoon from a seaplane with four household fans protruding from its sides. Despite its somewhat makeshift appearance, Maddock immediately recognized it for what it was—a diver propulsion vehicle, or DPV.

One more mystery solved, Maddock thought. He kicked harder, intent on intercepting the nearest diver before the man could reach the getaway ride, but as he stretched out his hand to rip the man's mask off, there was a flash from just beyond the DPV. A shaft of sickly yellow light stabbed out, transfixing Maddock in its glare.

A third diver. The treasure pirates had thought of everything, including a getaway driver.

Correctly interpreting the light as a warning signal, the diver with the chest turned away just as Maddock made his move. Maddock's fingers grazed the man's head but missed the mask straps. From the corner of his eye, he saw the diver let go of the chest, hands rising to block Maddock's attack. Maddock made another grab for the man's mask but the water slowed his movements just enough to allow the other man to catch his wrist. Maddock in turn caught the man's other hand and the two began a sort of slow motion dance, twisting and struggling, trying to gain an advantage, which was easier said than done. In the near-zero-gravity underwater environment, size and strength were of little value. Neither man could get the leverage needed to pull free of the other. Maddock's training in underwater hand-to-hand combat might have tipped the scales in his favor, if not for the fact that the odds against him were three-to-one.

Crap! Maddock thought as a figure emerged from behind the DPV, a large dive knife glinting in one outthrust hand.

The newcomer kicked forward, leading with the knife, like a human harpoon aimed straight at Maddock's heart. Maddock tried again to wrench his arm free, but the man holding him was tremendously strong—as strong as Bones, which was saying something. Then, as if in response to some prearranged signal, the man twisted around and stretched his arms out, holding Maddock spread-eagled, a perfect target for his buddy with the knife.

Maddock lost sight of the incoming blade, but he had a good sense of how far away the diver was and how long it would take him to cross that distance, so at the last instant before the attack, he released his opponent's wrist and twisted out of the way.

His human shield gone, the big diver let go of Maddock's wrist in a self-preservation reflex and pushed away from the incoming blade, its razor edge missing him by mere centimeters, even as the diver with the knife shifted direction to reacquire his target.

Maddock kicked a few feet away and turned to keep an eye on both men. By some unspoken agreement, the rogue treasure hunters moved away from each other, circling around Maddock in an obvious attempt to flank him. The man with the knife slashed it back and forth. The density of the water slowed his movements, depriving the gesture of any menace he might have hoped to project. Maddock guessed it was intended more as a distraction, a way to keep his attention diverted while the other diver tried to get behind him. Rather than let him do that, Maddock kicked forward, straight through the gap between them, like a minnow darting away from a predator, and then whirled around to face them.

It was a standoff, and one that might have gone on indefinitely, but just then, Maddock glimpsed another spot of light emerging from the murky darkness behind the men. Reinforcements were arriving, but for whom?

The light grew steadily brighter, bright enough that the treasure-pirates soon took note. The two men exchanged a few quick hand signals, then abruptly turned and began swimming furiously in the direction of the DPV. Even as they raced past, the source of the approaching light was revealed. Another diver emerged from the yellow murk, this one wearing a dry-suit almost identical to Maddock's own, only a few sizes larger.

Bones! And not a moment too soon.

Although the big Cherokee could not have known what was happening below the surface, he had come loaded for bear, or more precisely, barracuda. His massive hands held the 42-inch long tubular body of a JBL Magnum 38 Special Double Sling Spear Gun, and judging by the way his eyes were shifting back and forth behind his mask, he was looking for someone to shoot it at.

Maddock waved to get Bones' attention, and then pointed frantically at the retreating divers. The bigger of the pair—the one without the knife—was stooping to retrieve the chest. Bones gave the briefest of nods and then changed course, raising the spear gun meaningfully as he swam toward the looter. Maddock doubted his friend would actually use the weapon. With a single harpoon and an effective range of less than fifteen feet, it was designed for spear-fishing, not combat, but it was still a powerful deterrent.

The diver let go of the chest and then kicked his fins against the bottom, stirring up a veritable smokescreen of sediment to hide his escape.

Bones, evidently deciding that simply scaring them off wasn't good enough, decided to press his point by triggering the spear gun. The twin-barb Rockpoint tip harpoon shot through the water like a lightning bolt, vanishing into the dark cloud. Bones immediately pulled back on the attached line, retrieving the spear which had failed to find a flesh-and-blood target. He quickly returned the harpoon to the launch tube and braced the butt end against his chest in order to pull back the heavy-duty rubber slings, but Maddock waved him off before he could fire it again. He had no doubt that the divers were already long gone, whisked away by the DPV.

Without waiting for the silt cloud to diminish, Maddock kicked forward, aiming for the spot where the looter had dropped the chest. He groped blindly for a few seconds, feeling nothing but soft mud against his gloved hands, but then his fingers struck something hard and unyielding. He dug his fingers in around it, finding the edges and corners. It was so heavy that he had to plant his feet on the bottom in order to get enough leverage to lift it. Getting it to the surface would be a chore, but it was one he welcomed. The looter might have gotten the mask, but Bones' well-timed intervention had at least denied them one prize.

THREE

"**Sorry to disappoint** you, but I'm afraid this is not pirate booty."

The person on the other end of the line, and the source of this declaration was Amalia Oro, the Brazilian representative of the Global Heritage Commission and Maddock's point of contact for their current assignment. She spoke English fluently, but with a thick and somewhat jarring accent that challenged Maddock's ability to comprehend. After an earlier phone conversation, prior to making the voyage southward, Bones had remarked that she sounded like the actress Sofia Vergara, adding, "If she looks anything like her, then I'm definitely going to like this job, even if it means swimming in crap water."

Maddock had no idea what the woman looked like. All he really knew about her was what he had gleaned from browsing her *curriculum vitae* on the GHC website. After earning degrees in anthropology and South American history, Amalia had worked for many years as activist to protect the indigenous peoples of Brazil. Her current position with the United Nations agency focused on cultural and environmental issues relating to the Central Amazon Conservation Complex—one of the largest World Heritage Sites on the list. Although she was currently based in Rio de Janeiro, there had been neither opportunity nor reason for a face-to-face meeting. Their business thus far had been conducted electronically—mostly through email. This phone call had in fact been prompted by his last email correspondence, a brief account of his discovery at the wreck site and the subsequent assault by the looters, along with several pictures of the golden chest.

The artifact was smooth and undecorated, with a slight convex curve on one side—like a domed lid—though judging by the position of the small hook latch positioned in the exact center of one side panel, and the seam running vertically under it, it was more of a cabinet than a chest.

While he and Bones had been busy with decontamination procedures—which for Maddock now included a shower with strong disinfectant soap—Corey Dean had taken charge of the artifact, keeping it immersed in a tub of bay water while taking digital photographs of it from every possible angle. The call had come less than five minutes after Maddock sent the pictures to Amalia in an email attachment. As was his custom, Maddock had put the call on speaker phone so the rest of his crew could listen, ask questions, and add their insights.

"So what is it, then?" Maddock asked, glancing over at the tub and its contents.

"If I'm not mistaken" Amalia said, "it is a Christian reliquary. A chest for holding and transporting holy relics. Most likely from the early colonial period."

"But it could still be pirate treasure, couldn't it?" Bones challenged. "Maybe pirates ransacked a church and stole this."

"Yes, that is possible. I only meant that you should not expect it to be full of gold coins and gemstones. I don't know if you are aware of this but every Catholic church has a holy relic of some kind, however small or insignificant. Pieces of the cross, fingerbones of saints.

That sort of thing."

"The knife Elvis used to make his peanut butter and banana sandwiches," Bones quipped.

Amalia didn't hear him. "The reliquary itself is probably of more intrinsic value than whatever is inside." She paused a beat before adding. "I am actually more interested in the mask you mentioned. From your description, it sounds more like a native headdress than a sacred Church relic."

There was a faint tapping sound across the line and then she spoke again. "I am sending you an email. Tell me if it resembles what you saw."

Maddock turned to his laptop and found the email with the attached picture—a photograph of a man, an indigenous tribesman judging by the streaks of ritual paint on his mocha-colored skin and the bright red feather which protruded from his pierced septum. The man also wore a headdress of blue feathers which were fanned out in a circle around the crown of his head.

"Very similar," Maddock answered. "Except what I found also had a mask that would have completely covered the eyes of someone wearing it. No eyeholes."

"A mask with no eye holes? Very interesting." There were more tapping sounds, but Amalia offered no further comment.

"I didn't think the natives in this region worked with metals," observed Matt Barnaby, another member of the *Sea Foam* crew, who had been half-listening to the conversation as he scanned the surrounding waters with a pair of binoculars, hoping to get lucky and spot the boat from which the treasure hunting pirates were operating. Lean and rangy, Matt had been a ground-pounding Army Ranger before teaming up with

Maddock for adventures on the high seas, and while he was a capable enough marine salvage engineer, his skill with a rifle often proved of greater practical value.

"To the best of our knowledge, they did not," Amalia admitted. "It is a mystery, and one we may not be able to solve without recovering the artifact itself. It's a pity you weren't able to retrieve it."

"That's not the word I would use," Maddock said, anger flaring at the memory of the lost artifact.

"Save your pity for the guys who took it," Bones growled. "When I find them, I'm going to rip their arms off and beat them to death with them."

To Maddock's surprise, the gruesome remark elicited mild laughter on the other end of the line. "I think I'd like to take a swing or two myself."

"Speaking of which," Maddock said, "Has there been any progress on that front?"

"I've passed your report on to the Federal Police. They'll be watching to see if the artifact turns up on the black market. We may get lucky, but I wouldn't count on it."

"These guys were pros. They knew what they were doing down there, and they had the equipment to pull it off. There can't be that many salvage operators working down here."

"They knew we were here and what we were doing," put in Willis Sanders, the fifth member of the crew. The sun glistened on the crown of his dark, shaved head. Sanders had been a SEAL teammate of Maddock and Bones, and had followed along when they embarked on their new adventure as treasure hunters. "Maybe they're out-of-towners, too."

"It's possible. I expect the Federal Police will want to

question you further."

Maddock was surprised that had not already happened, and was frankly dreading it. If past experience was any guide, law enforcement officials were rarely sympathetic to treasure hunters, even when they were the aggrieved party. "So, what do you want us to do now? Should we keep searching this wreck or move on?"

"For the moment, I would suggest we focus on the reliquary. While it may not exactly be what the Brazilian government expected, it may still be a significant discovery. I will inquire with the Archdiocese as well. Meanwhile, there is a conservation laboratory at the University campus on Ilha do Fundão. Do you know where that is?"

Maddock recognized the name of the large island in the North Zone of Rio. "Sure. It's only about ten miles from here."

"I will email you the exact address. Bring the reliquary. I will meet you there, say at six tonight?"

"Six is good," Bones said before Maddock could answer. "Maybe after that, we can ditch Maddock, and then you can show me what a good time in Rio looks like."

Even though he was accustomed to Bones' desperate and pathetically misguided attempts to impress every woman he encountered, Maddock winced a little. Amalia wasn't just some random encounter at a dive bar. She was, for all intents and purposes, their employer, and making a bad impression might not only sour their current working relationship but close the door on future opportunities.

But if she took offense, Amalia gave no indication. Instead, she simply chuckled again and then said, "It's

Mr. Breakbones, right?"

Bones grinned but did not correct her. "Just call me Bones."

"Bones, do you know what today is?"

Bones was momentarily taken aback, though whether it was the question or simply the fact that he had not been rejected out of hand, Maddock couldn't say. "Uh, not really. TGI Friday?"

"Tonight, Carnaval begins. I don't think we will have any trouble finding a good time for you."

FOUR

Even though it was still early, the white beaches and streets of Copacabana were already crowded with people getting a head start on the five-day-long exercise in excess known as Carnaval, and Sam Decker was eager to join their ranks.

Like most of the scantily clad, more-than-a-little-inebriated men and women currently gyrating to the strains of live samba music around him, Decker cared little about the Lenten season—the six-weeks of self-induced depravation that would ostensibly follow the much briefer period of debauchery. He didn't need a reason to party, but tonight, he actually had one. The golden mask, which he and his crew had snatched out from under the nose of that boy scout, Dane Maddock, would pay off his outstanding debts, with enough left over to keep him and his men in *cachaça* and *senhoritas* until it was time to head back to the Keys.

He was just about to start pushing through the crowd in search of a bar when he felt a hand close around his left bicep. "*Senhor Decker.*"

Decker's free hand immediately sought out his trouser pocket, where he kept a meticulously honed stiletto, but he stopped short of actually drawing the spring-loaded, folding blade. This was no place for a knife fight, and besides, if this was who he thought it was, then it was nobody he wanted to cross. Forcing himself to relax, stilling his face to calm, he turned his head to face his assailant. "Yes?"

The man was about the same height as Decker's

ironically-nicknamed first mate, Tiny, but built like a sumo wrestler. Pudgy cheeks forced his lips into a permanent sneer, but underneath all that blubber was solid muscle. Decker could tell that much just from the iron grip on his arm. Powerful fingers dug into his flesh, but he did not wince. He wouldn't show weakness. "He wishes to speak with you. This way, *senhor*."

Decker's mouth went suddenly dry. There was little question about who *he* was.

Without waiting for consent, the man drew him back out of the crowd and steered him toward a side-street where a black limousine waited. The big man opened the rear door and propelled Decker inside, where he found his employer seated and waiting.

Decker straightened in the chair, making an effort to reclaim at least some of his dignity. "Fancy meeting you here. Come for Carnaval?"

Cardinal Sergio Ribeiro regarded him with a dour expression, though Decker couldn't recall ever seeing him look otherwise. Although dressed simply in black clerical attire, his demeanor alone sufficed to convey the authority of his office. "I think you know precisely why I'm here."

"News travels fast, huh?" In fact, it had only been a couple hours since his little snatch-and-grab, and just twenty or so minutes since he'd tied up his boat, *Opportunity Aknockin',* at a nearby marina. "You know, you didn't need to come down here to thank me in person."

"*Thank* you?" Ribeiro almost spat the words out. "I hired you to keep an eye on Maddock, not assault him."

Decker shrugged. "We got lucky. Look, I had to make a judgment call. He had found something.

Something valuable."

"And so you took it. Like a common pirate." Ribeiro's expression said just what he thought of pirates.

"Not *like*," Decker said, flashing a grin. "You knew what I was when you hired me. But I'll tell you what. Since I was technically working for you, it's only fair that I let you bid first."

"Bid?" The cardinal retorted, one white eyebrow arched incredulously.

"It's a nice piece. The gold alone is probably worth a couple hundred grand."

"As you were operating in my employ," Ribeiro hissed, "Anything you recover would automatically become my property."

Decker kept his grin in place. "I suppose you could make a case for that in a court of law, but are you sure you want to go on record with that? Seems much simpler to just pay me for it. God knows, you've got the cash." He winked. "Pun very much intended."

The older man regarded him silently, contemptuously, for several seconds, long enough that Decker started to wonder if he had overplayed his hand. The cardinal was a very powerful man. He was not merely above the law—the law was beholden to him. Political officials served at his whim. Industrial giants actively sought his favor. And he had a reputation for ruthlessness that Decker suspected was well-deserved. If he wanted, Ribeiro could instruct his hulking bodyguard to crush Decker into a little ball and drop him in the bay, and neither of them would lose any sleep worrying about the consequences in this life or the one to come.

"Look, all I'm asking is fair market value—"

Ribeiro cut him off. "Describe it to me."

"What?"

"The artifact you… 'liberated', from Mr. Maddock. Tell me about it."

"Looks like some kind of fancy hat. A crown maybe." He brought his hands up to either side of his head, fingers splayed like the rays of a sunrise. "It's got these points. Feathers, maybe. And it's gold. Can't speak to the purity, but the sucker weighs fifteen… maybe twenty pounds."

"A crown." Ribeiro's eyes seemed to lose focus, as if distracted by a memory. "Could it be a mask?"

Decker shrugged. "I suppose. If you turned it around backwards and poked a couple holes to see through."

The cardinal's gaze snapped back to him. "There should have been something else with it. A chest about so big." He held his hands up, about twelve inches between them.

Roughly the same dimensions as the chest they had taken from the wreck, and which Tiny had dropped during the struggle with Dane Maddock.

Striving for his best poker face, Decker replied, "No, I didn't see anything like that, but it could still be down there. I can go back for it if you like. Could be a little risky, though, especially now that Maddock knows he's not the only one looking."

The cardinal opened his mouth to reply but then stopped, and instead reached into the folds of his cassock and withdrew a mobile phone. An audible hum issued from the device as it vibrated in his hands. He glanced at the illuminated screen for a moment, then hit a button to receive an incoming call.

He spoke in Portuguese. Decker, who spoke a smattering of Spanish, understood most of what he heard, but Ribeiro's side of the conversation was too brief for him to grasp the subject. As the call went on, the older man's gaze drifted back to Decker and his expression changed noticeably. Decker heard him thank the person on the other end of the line and then he ended the call. When he returned his attention to Decker, he was almost smiling.

"Good news, *Senhor* Decker. I think I can help expedite your search."

FIVE

The non-stop party atmosphere of Carnaval held little attraction for Maddock, which made him the odd man out among his crew, so he promised the others that, as soon as the business at the conservation lab was concluded, he would return to *Sea Foam* and stand watch while the rest of them enjoyed a little shore leave. After what had happened at the dive site, he didn't want to leave the boat unguarded, so Willis—loser of the coin-flip with Matt—remained behind with Corey, while Bones and Matt accompanied Maddock ashore at Fundão Island.

The artificially created island, also known as Cidade Universitária—College City—was already bustling with activity as young people—students and tourists alike—filled the streets in celebration, but Maddock succeeded in hailing a taxi to bear them from the moorage to the address Amalia had provided.

For ease of transport, they had transferred the heavy chest into a large plastic bag filled with sea water, which was in turn sealed inside a bag normally reserved for diving equipment. Maintaining immersion was probably an unnecessary step, but Maddock figured it was better to let the conservation technicians at the University make that determination. That way, no one could blame him if the contents turned out to be nothing but decomposed mush.

As they entered the lobby of the building, they were met by a woman who, if she swapped her professional-looking business suit for a string bikini, might easily have passed for one of the students cavorting outside. With an oval face framed by long, straight honey-colored hair, she probably could have had a lucrative career on the fashion runway or in front of the camera.

She stepped forward to greet them, her gaze shifting between their faces. "Mr. Maddock?"

If he had any doubt that this was indeed Amalia Oro, the voice—and the accent—swept it away. But before he could acknowledge or accept her handclasp, Bones stepped forward quickly.

"Maddock is the pipsqueak holding the bag. I'm the guy you really want to talk to."

Maddock sighed. At an even six feet in height, Maddock could hardly be called short, but Bones nevertheless delighted in pointing out the difference in their height, particularly when there was an attractive woman within earshot.

"Mr. Breakbones?" Amalia flashed him a dazzling smile as she let her gaze roll up and down him. "You surprise me. Usually it is the littlest dogs that bark the loudest."

Behind him, Matt Barnaby let out a snort of laughter. "There's all different kinds of little."

Bones shot him a look that would have turned Medusa to stone. "Nice, dude. I'll remember that."

Maddock stepped forward, eager to put the meeting back on track. "Dr. Oro, I'm Dane Maddock. And this—" He held up the bag. "Is what we found. Where do you want it?"

"I'm no doctor, Mr. Maddock. Please, just call me Amalia." She gave Bones another long, teasing look. "I guess you can, too." Then she gestured to the hallway behind her. "This way."

After a couple of turns, they entered a large, well-lit, open room. There were several worktables arrayed throughout, many of them occupied with projects in various states of progress. A few sported what looked at a glance like large fish tanks. There was only one other person in the room however, a handsome, well-groomed, young man wearing a lab coat, who turned to greet them as they stepped inside.

The man, Ricardo wasted no time removing the reliquary from Maddock's bag and placing it on his table where he began inspecting it under a large, swivel-mounted, illuminated, magnifying lens. After studying it from every angle, he opened the sealed plastic bag and drained the contents. Even after the bag was emptied, water continued to dribble from the reliquary, seeping out through the seams.

"It opens at the front, here." Ricardo said. He used a metal probe to point out the vertical seam, and then followed it up to where it intersected a barely visible horizontal line just below the start of the curve at the top. "It does not appear to be water-tight, so whatever is inside has been immersed for…" He shrugged. "I would guess at least three or four centuries." He paused a moment, then added, "I will open it now."

Maddock unconsciously held his breath as the technician used the probe to lift the metal hook securing the door panels. He half expected the doors to burst open of their own accord, but they did not even budge, even when Ricardo gently teased them with the probe. Abandoning the cautious approach, he reached out with both hands—both covered in a pair of latex examination gloves—and applied direct force. The doors swung open on recessed hinges, releasing what water remained inside the chest in a single, vomitous discharge. Unable to restrain his curiosity, Maddock leaned down and looked inside.

The reliquary was empty.

"Holy crap," Bones muttered.

Ricardo moved the magnifying lens lower so that its light shone into the empty interior of the reliquary.

It was immediately evident that the gold panels on the exterior were not solely responsible for the artifact's considerable weight. In fact, the gold layer was relatively thin, the soft metal hammered into sheets and pressed into place over an inner structure, an open cube with sides more than an inch thick—like the walls of a heavy-duty safe. The material comprising the inner compartment was a dark gray stone with distinctive angular fracture planes suggesting a tabular crystalline structure. The irregularities caught and reflected the light from the magnifying lens to dazzling effect. The inner hollow was only about eight inches across, and seemed to have been carved out of a solid block of the mineral.

"Just a big block of rock," Bones muttered.

Amalia must have read Maddock's equally dismayed expression. "Don't be disappointed. The reliquary itself may be the real treasure. Perhaps it was used to transport a holy relic from the Old World to one of the first churches in Brazil."

Maddock offered a desultory shrug. "That's not exactly the headline grabber you were looking for, though."

"Might be more like it on the wreck," Bones suggested.

Amalia nodded equivocally. "I have asked a historian from the archdiocese to examine the reliquary. They may be able to determine more about its actual history. Perhaps even the name of the ship. We should probably wait for that before determining how best to proceed."

"Cool," Bones said. "Then we're done here. I seem to recall something about a carnival?"

Ricardo's enthusiastic grin indicated that Bones wasn't the only person in the room eager to party, but Maddock wasn't ready to throw in the towel. "I wish we could have held onto that mask. I can't help but think the two are related."

"Mask?" Ricardo said, taking an interest.

Amalia shifted uncomfortably. She evidently had not shared that part of the story with the technician. Maddock gave her a questioning look, to which she responded with a nod. "I found this next to what looked like a gold mask, fashioned to resemble a native headdress."

"*A máscara não tinha olhos*," Amalia added in Portuguese.

Maddock was fluent in Spanish, and the two languages were similar enough for him to get the gist of what she had said. *The mask has no eyes.* He thought it unusual that she had chosen to emphasize that detail to the technician in their preferred tongue, but evidently Ricardo immediately grasped the significance. "*¿Sem olhos? ¿Como o caso das máscaras de chumbo?*"

"*Sim. Exatamente.*"

"Hey, watch your language," Bones grumbled, voicing Maddock's own irritation at being left out of the conversation.

Amalia smiled but her expression remained wary, as if the subject was one she was hesitant to explore. "We are just saying that the mask you found reminds us of a story… I think you would call it a… An urban myth? Is that the term."

Maddock nodded. "What's the connection?"

"We call it *O Caso das Máscaras de Chumbo*. The Lead Masks Case. It was many years ago—"

"Nineteen sixty-six," supplied Ricardo.

"*Sim*," Amalia said, with a nod of gratitude. "Two bodies were found on a hill in Niterói on the other side of the bay. Two men, wearing formal suits, but over them, raincoats and on their faces, they wore masks made of lead over their eyes. Masks with no eye holes."

"Masks and raincoats," Bones remarked. "Sounds like your kind of kink, Matt."

Matt smirked. Bones was making good on his promise to retaliate for Matt's earlier jibe, which meant, for the moment at least Maddock was no longer the target of opportunity.

Amalia continued with her story. "The police also found an empty, metal water bottle and a note with instructions for the men. The note told them to swallow a pill, and then when it took effect, to put on the mask and wait."

"So what killed them?" Maddock asked. "The pills?"

"No one is certain. For some reason, the autopsy was delayed, and by the time the tests were performed, the organs were already too badly decayed to determine cause of death. But there were no other signs of trauma, so poison is the most likely explanation."

Maddock had never heard the story and wondered if Amalia was recalling the details correctly, or if perhaps it was, as she had first suggested, just an urban legend.

"Many say they were trying to contact aliens," Ricardo put in.

He was smiling when he said it, but Bones' ears immediately perked up. "Aliens?"

"*Sim.* That place, Morro do Vintém, near Niteroi, has many sightings of UFOs."

"Maybe they were waiting for a spaceship that didn't come," Maddock suggested. "Like the Heaven's Gate suicide cult."

Amalia nodded. "That is the more plausible theory. Anyway, I'm sure it doesn't have anything to do with the mask you found. I was just remarking on the similarity."

"Well, hold on," Bones interjected. "It raises a good question. Why make a mask with no eye-holes? Are there any pictures of these lead masks?"

As if anticipating the request, Ricardo had his smartphone out and after a couple seconds of entering information, turned the screen to show a black and white image of two crude-looking eye masks. The image was clearly old, a grainy newspaper photograph, but to Maddock, the "masks" looked like someone had wrapped a pair of horn-rimmed glasses in metal foil.

"Those don't look anything like the mask I found," he said.

"Maybe not," Bones persisted, "But why wear a mask? A lead mask? With no eyeholes? I can only think of one reason."

"To protect your eyes from radiation," Matt supplied.

"I was going to say 'In case Maddock takes off his shirt in front of you,'" Bones shot back, grinning, "but I guess it's kind of the same thing."

Amalia now wore a pinched expression, as if regretting having mentioned the mystery at all. Ricardo however seemed to be enjoying himself. "There is another theory that the men may have been planning to buy nuclear materials. Both men were electronics technicians from Campos dos Goytacazes, almost three hundred kilometers away. They told their families they were going to purchase supplies. Maybe supplies to build an atom bomb?"

"What would a couple electricians from the boonies want with a nuke?" asked Bones.

"That was a difficult time in my country," Amalia explained. "There were many left-wing revolutionaries who wanted to overthrow the government. A military coup had taken over in 1964. They committed many human rights abuses. Kidnapping, torture, even rape and castration of prisoners."

Bones grimaced.

"It may be that these men believed they could build an atom bomb," Ricardo said. "They may have been attempting to procure the necessary material, but someone betrayed them. Poisoned them. It may even have been a…"

He hesitated as if searching for the word. Bone supplied it. "A set-up?"

"*Sim.*"

"That explains your lead mask mystery," Maddock said, "But it doesn't have anything to do with a gold mask from a four-hundred-year-old shipwreck." He paused a beat, then added, "Unless you think the local Indians were trying to nuke the Portuguese colonists?"

"I'm sure they would have liked to," Amalia said, with a relieved smile. "But you are right. There is no connection. Just a coincidence."

Bones still wasn't ready to let go of it. He turned to Maddock. "Remember when we were looking for the

Liberty Bell 7 capsule and found that old Spanish wreck? It was carrying radioactive ore that had been found here. In South America. They didn't even know what uranium *was* back then. It was just a weird rock to them, but they took it anyway."

"That may be true, but it's still a long way from saying that the natives figured out safe handling procedures for nuclear material."

"Dude, we both know the early American cultures were a lot more sophisticated than they get credit for. We have a wide range of talents." Bones said, with a glance to Amalia, as if hoping to impress her with his range of knowledge. Her expression however revealed more confusion than anything else.

Bones wasn't wrong though. They had encountered evidence aplenty of ancient so-called primitive cultures with access to science that was, even by modern standards, cutting edge. Maddock bent low to have another look at the reliquary. "Let's say, for the sake of argument that these masks—gold and lead—served the same purpose as radiation shields. How does this fit in?"

Amalia's eyes grew as big as saucers and she took a big step back. "Is it radioactive?"

Ricardo looked at it a little nervously as well, but Matt spoke up quickly to alleviate their concerns. "Not likely. I don't think it's uranium or any other radioactive metal, but even if it is, you can't get a lethal dose from short term exposure to naturally occurring radioactive ores."

"What if it's not naturally occurring?" Bones pointed out, putting a protective arm out in front of Amalia as if his biceps could block gamma rays.

Matt glared at him. "Thanks for backing me up,

dude."

Maddock did not back away from the reliquary. Instead, he reached in with a bare finger and touched the gray crystalline material inside. "I don't think it's radioactive, but it could be part of some kind of primitive radiological weapon. It might be a good idea to figure out what it actually is. And why someone decided to turn it into a reliquary." He frowned, straightening. "Of course, we don't even know if there is a connection between the mask and the reliquary."

"The man who hired me to get them seemed to think there's a connection."

The unfamiliar voice from behind them caused everyone to turn and look, but Maddock's instincts were already flashing with a warning message. He didn't recognize the two men standing just inside the entrance—one of them short and stocky, the other a hulking brute almost as tall as Bones—but the guns they held pointed casually in the direction of the group inside the lab confirmed that his instincts were spot on.

SIX

Amalia and Ricardo reacted as anyone would, with a mixture of shock, fear and denial, but Maddock and his crew remained cool. It wasn't the first time someone had pointed a gun at them, and Maddock knew it wouldn't be the last. The fact that the gunmen had announced their presence with words rather than bullets was a pretty good indication that outright violence wasn't their preferred option. That gave Maddock a little room to maneuver.

"You guys lost?" Bones said. "The party's outside."

The two gunmen were certainly dressed for the festivities. They wore Bermuda shorts, loud, short-sleeved shirts in a faux-African tribal pattern and bright blue, straw trilby hats, which seemed to be the preferred headgear of Carnaval. Both were Caucasian, and judging by the accent of the man who had just spoken, not local. Almost certainly Americans.

"You must be the guys who took the mask," Maddock said.

The smaller man laughed. "Brilliant deduction, Sherlock. Now, all of you, move over there." He waggled the barrel of the gun to the left of the lab table. "And don't get any crazy ideas about trying to play hero. You got lucky this morning, but it won't happen again."

Bones cocked his head sideways, eyes narrowing at the stocky figure. "You look familiar. Have we met?"

The man laughed. "Not counting this morning? I don't think so. But I know all about you two Boy Scouts."

Bones snapped his fingers. "Of course. It wasn't you.

Just something that looked like you." He turned to Amalia. "Maddock left his tighty-whiteys in the head. There was a skid mark that looked exactly like that guy." He glanced over his shoulder at the larger man. "Though come to think of it, maybe it looked more like him."

"Funny guy," said the smaller man. "You should do stand-up. You could probably get hired by the tribe to do shows at a casino. All those drunk Indians will really yuk it up."

"That's not a bad idea," Bones replied, without missing a beat. "I could do the whole Gallagher routine. And you could be my watermelon."

"I don't get it," muttered the bigger man.

"Shut up," his partner snarled. "Quit jerkin' around and move."

But Bones did not move. "Come on guys, the least you can do is introduce yourselves." He half-turned to Maddock. "I really do recognize these guys. Little stain there is Sam Decker. The big pile of crap next to him goes by 'Tiny,' because… You know, irony."

Maddock recognized the names if not the faces. Sam Decker was notorious in the Florida Keys as a two-bit confidence man, smuggler and reputed treasure-pirate. But not a killer.

"Decker," he murmured. "You know you're right. He does look like a skid mark." He sniffed. "Smells like one, too."

"Dude, you sniff your skid marks?" Bones asked.

Decker jabbed the gun forward, forcefully. "Last warning! Move it."

Maddock was certain that Decker wouldn't pull the trigger, at least not intentionally, but he complied, taking a couple steps to the left, clearing the path for the two hoodlums. As he did, he continued speaking. "So, you followed us all the way from Key West, just hoping we'd find something so you could loot our claim? Congratulations on taking a big step up in the world, Decker. You're now an international criminal."

"I don't think anyone's gonna be pressin' charges, Maddock. My employer will take care of that."

"And who might that be? If he wanted the artifacts, he could have just dealt with me directly."

"Nice try. But I'll tell him. Maybe he will *deal* with you."

Maddock glanced over at Bones. "Was that supposed to be a threat? I can't tell."

Bones shrugged. "Maybe you have to find someone intimidating before it can have an effect." He glanced at Amalia. "What was that you were saying about little dogs?"

Despite the fear in her eyes, the comment caused the corners of her mouth to twitch.

The still-fuming Decker turned to his accomplice. "Tiny, get the box. I'll cover you."

The brutish Tiny nodded and jammed his gun into the waistband of his shorts before advancing to scoop the reliquary up, holding it in the crook of his elbow. He turned to face his boss, a look of satisfaction on his otherwise dull face.

Decker rolled his eyes. "For Chrissake, Tiny. Put it in a bag or somethin'."

Chastened, the big man turned until he spotted Maddock's dive bag resting on the ground beside the table. Without setting the artifact down, he retrieved the bag and then began awkwardly trying to shove the former into the latter. As the comical struggle stretched out for more than a minute, the sound of crickets chirping inexplicably filled the air.

After another minute of fighting with the inanimate objects, Tiny succeeded, zipping the bag shut with a flourish. "Hah! Did it!"

Bones started clapping excitedly. "Amazing! Decker, give him a banana!"

The big goon glowered and took a menacing step toward Bones.

"Tiny!" Decker barked. "Forget him. We've got what we came for."

He inclined his head toward the exit and then began backing toward it, his pistol pointed in the general direction of Maddock and the others, his aim shifting from one person to the next at random intervals. He stopped beside the door, urging Tiny to leave first, and then backed through quickly and was gone.

It had not escaped Maddock's notice that the two looters had not searched them for weapons or phones, or made any other effort to restrain them.

"Talk about comedy routines," Bones muttered, shaking his head.

"Not exactly a pair of criminal masterminds," agreed Maddock. "Guess we better go after them."

Amalia eyed them both. "What are you talking about? We should call the police."

"You heard what he said," Bones replied. "He's got some kind of pull with the local authorities."

"Call them," Maddock called out, starting for the exit. aware that Bones was right behind him. "But I'm going after Decker."

As he left the lab, he was moving at a jog, which he hoped would be just fast enough to catch up to Decker as he left the building. He didn't want to overtake the escaping pair inside, where there was no room to maneuver, but neither did he want to let them get too much of a head start. He quickened his step when the main entrance came into view, the doors just swinging shut.

He burst through the exit and saw Decker and Tiny striding purposefully toward the street. They were easy to spot, especially with Tiny towering above everyone else. Maddock immediately saw where they were headed however, and knew that their loud attire would actually serve as camouflage once they reached their immediate destination.

The crowd filling the streets in anticipation of the Carnaval celebration had more than doubled in size during the brief time they'd spent examining the reliquary. Even as Maddock accelerated to a sprint, he saw the escaping men disappear into a group of similarly dressed young people, swaying to the frenetic rhythms of samba music that was pounding across the campus at near-deafening decibel levels.

"When you mentioned Carnaval," Bones shouted, "I thought we'd have to go to it, not the other way around."

The comment was just odd enough that Maddock glanced over his shoulder. Bones hadn't been talking to him, but rather to Amalia, who along with Matt and Ricardo, had followed him from the lab.

Maddock frowned. He had hoped that the two Brazilians would stay behind, perhaps wait for the police to show up. He didn't need the added distraction of having to worry about their safety. Still, another couple pairs of eyes might come in handy, and he had no doubt that Bones would make Amalia's safety a priority.

Which meant he could focus entirely on stopping Decker.

He angled toward the spot where he'd last seen the two men and plunged into the crowd, shouting, "Coming through!" He didn't know how to say it in Portuguese, but figured even the non-English speakers would get the point. Most did, and moved aside, albeit grudgingly, and as he jostled through their midst, he saw the crown of a bright blue trilby hat floating above a sea of bobbing heads, just a few yards ahead.

Not wanting to give himself away, Maddock stopped shouting and snaked through the crowd, ducking under waving arms. He felt a splash of something lukewarm on his back and immediately smelled the distinctive sour, tangy odor of beer. The spill had probably been intentional, payback for having bumped someone in the crowd a little too forcefully, but Maddock didn't have time to deal with the slight.

The crowd was densest on the sidewalk running along a main thoroughfare, but just beyond, a long row of wooden barricades formed a boundary to prevent their revelry from overflowing onto the pavement. Just beyond the barrier, scores of figures dressed in elaborate, and in many cases, very revealing costumes, were lined up in a quasi-military formation, moving down the street, half-marching, half-dancing to the music. It was one of Rio's famous samba school parades, a precursory event to the elaborate and highly competitive event that would begin the following day at the Sambadrome Marquês de Sapucaí, just a few miles away. Even at this small scale, it was a dazzling spectacle and a little distracting, but after a moment of searching, Maddock again spotted his quarry moving up the street threading between the barricades and the crowd. He gave chase, pushing past revelers, closing on the two men who remained unaware of the pursuit. At first, the throng of spectators hampered his efforts, but as he got closer, he was able to slip into the temporary void left in Tiny's wake, and he was able to cross the last five yards at a full sprint.

The big man, trusting his prodigious strength, had opted to simply hold the bag by its carry handles, letting it hang low at his side, rather than slinging it over one shoulder to more easily distribute the heavy burden, which made it relatively simple for Maddock to strip the bag out of his grip simply by throwing his full weight onto it.

The unexpected move pulled Tiny off balance, causing him to topple forward, faceplanting on the pavement at Decker's heels. The impact broke his grip, allowing Maddock to spring up, his prize cradled in both arms against his chest, and run back in the direction from which he'd come.

Unfortunately, the crowd had already filled in behind him, covering the trail he'd blazed through their midst. He could see Bones' head above the crowd, just twenty yards away, but getting through the mass of writhing humanity without being able to use his hands was going to be a challenge. Like a quarterback trying a goal line sneak, he battled against the mass of human bodies that impeded his progress.

"Bones!" He shouted. "I need an exit."

He couldn't tell if his friend had heard him over the noise, so he tried again. "Bones! I need—"

His shout was cut off, the air driven from his lungs by the impact of something—more likely someone—

plowing into him from behind. He stumbled forward into the mass of bodies, which broke his fall but did not prevent it completely, and slammed down atop the relic. Stunned and gasping for breath, he tightened his hold on the bag, but was unable to offer much resistance when his assailant grabbed his shoulder and flipped him over onto his back. Decker loomed over him, his face twisted in a snarl of rage. Maddock glimpsed a flash of motion, Decker's fist rocketing toward his face. Even if he had wanted to, Maddock knew there simply wasn't enough time for him to let go of the bag and block the incoming punch. All he could do was tuck his chin into his chest, rolling his head sideways to meet the incoming blow with his forehead.

A blue flash exploded across Maddock's vision, followed almost instantly by a loud ringing sound. There was pain, too, but not as much as he would have felt if Decker had connected with his jaw, or for that matter, as much as Decker was probably feeling; the bone in the human forehead was a lot tougher than the bones of the human hand. Through his disorientation, Maddock thought he could hear the other man swearing angrily.

But it had nevertheless been a solid hit, enough to make Maddock temporarily loosen his grip on the bag. He felt it slip through his arms, the weight of the reliquary vanishing. He struggled back to his feet, a railroad spike of pain stabbing through his head, and saw Decker's retreating back, the bag slung over one shoulder.

This time however, Decker wasn't going to take his chances muscling through the crowd. Instead, he slipped between two barricades, and burst out onto the street. Shouts of protest and dismay pierced through the cloud of ambient noise, and one or two concerned spectators ventured out after him, trying to pull him back. Decker had, no doubt, intended to slip into the gap between two groups of marching samba dancers, but the interference from the parade-viewers threw his timing off by a second or two, just long enough for the gap to close. Instead of sliding past the dancers, Decker careened into them, scattering scantily-clad bodies like bowling pins.

The disruption threw the crowd into an uproar. Maddock, who was still trying to shake off the effects of Decker's punch, was just about to head into the street after him when the throng surged forward around him. Reeling, he almost went down, but then felt a hand reach out to steady him.

"Maddock!" Bones barked at him. "You okay?"

Maddock nodded, and then regretted doing so. "Ow," he grimaced as pain shot through his head. "I'll live."

He glanced over at Bones, saw that Amalia was right beside him. On the street, Decker was just emerging from the scrum, with Maddock's bag now slung over his shoulder.

"Come on," Maddock urged, starting forward. "We can still get him."

But as he broke past the barricades, he heard Amalia shriek. "*Atento!*"

From the corner of his eye, he spotted a figure charging to intercept him—not a well-intentioned spectator, but Decker's brutish sidekick. The warning came too late for Maddock to do much of anything except mentally prepare for a collision that would make the hit from Decker seem like a gentle bump by comparison, but in the instant before contact, Maddock heard a sickening crunch as a second, smaller figure slammed into Tiny, knocking him off course. The big man stumbled, veering in front of Maddock, to ultimately crash into the tangled mass of samba dancers. A millisecond later, Matt Barnaby sprawled headlong on the pavement right in front of Maddock.

Maddock barely had time to leap over the prone and writhing shape of his friend. He resisted the impulse to stop and check the extent of Matt's injuries. The former Army Ranger would pay a steep price for the flying tackle, but if Maddock failed to bring Decker to heel, that sacrifice would count for nothing.

Thirty feet away, Decker had succeeded in extracting himself from the shattered ranks of the samba revue, and was up and running again, heading back up the street on the opposite side, in the same direction he had been going before. Maddock cut to the right, angling into the now widening gap that Decker had just missed, and charged after the escaping thief. Bones appeared beside him, keeping pace effortlessly. He glanced over at Maddock with a fierce grin. "I'm going to do a runaround. Watch for me."

Maddock flashed an upraised thumb, and Bones immediately pivoted, angling back toward the barricades behind them. Maddock now realized that Amalia was following him. She glanced back at Bones retreating form, then quickened her step to catch up with Maddock.

"Where's he going?" she said, half-gasping from the exertion of running.

"Never mind us," Maddock shot back. "Just find somewhere safe and wait for the police."

Maddock didn't wait for a reply but returned his

gaze to Decker's retreating form and poured on the speed. The thief was threading the narrow space between the barricades and another dance troupe, this one surrounding a large parade float upon which dozens more performers danced and cavorted high above the crowd.

The heavy artifact was clearly slowing Decker's pace, but not as much as the close confines. The samba dancers were shuffling from side-to-side, arms outflung and waving, completely unaware of the figure moving beside them, and not inclined to stop their performance in any event. Maddock had similar difficulty navigating past them, but unencumbered as he was, he managed to close to within fifteen feet of the thief before the latter reached the end of the float procession and broke into the open. That was when Bones stepped into the man's path, arms akimbo.

Decker made a last-ditch attempt to dodge around the big man, but there wasn't enough room for him to maneuver, and as he tried, Bones reached out and seized hold of the collar of Decker's obnoxious shirt, stopping him in his tracks and nearly yanking him off his feet.

Maddock arrived a moment later and, without breaking stride, hooked his arm through the sling of the dive bag and yanked it clear of the thief. The transfer of weight almost pulled him off balance, but he recovered on the run, angling in front of the dancers, making for the other side of the street.

As he rounded the corner of the procession, he cut to the right and headed back down the opposite side of the float, moving against the flow this time. The samba group had continued to advance, but the group behind them remained stalled after the collision with Decker and Tiny, creating an ever-widening gap, and worse, a swelling mass of humanity as curious spectators began moving up from further down the street.

Amalia was standing almost exactly where Maddock had last seen her, evidently refusing to take his advice. As soon as she spotted him, she began moving in his direction, waving her arms to get his attention. "*Senhor* Maddock! Over here."

Frowning at her stubbornness, he shifted to meet her. "Amalia. Come on. We need to get out of here."

Suddenly, a scream pierced through the tumult behind her. Maddock looked past to see people—dancers and spectators alike—parting like the sea in a Biblical miracle and fleeing for the relative safety of the sidewalk. As they cleared away, the cause of the sudden panic was revealed. Decker's sidekick Tiny stood in the middle of the emptying street, gun raised and searching for a target….

Finding one.

A hungry but giddy expression crossed the big brute's face as the barrel of the pistol swung toward Maddock.

Maddock grabbed Amalia's hand and spun around, dragging her along as he fled back up the street, trying to put the parade float between them and Tiny. He didn't want to believe that the big man would open fire in a crowd, but it was plainly evident that Decker had not hired him for his brains. Or his conscience. He was Decker's attack dog, and now, he was off leash.

A loud, distinctive report cracked through the din, triggering a fresh wave of panic that overtook Maddock and Amalia. The sound did not repeat. If Tiny's intent had been to frighten the crowd, scattering them out of the way, it had backfired. Maddock and Amalia were caught up in the stampede, swept around the slow-moving float like flotsam in a raging river.

For several seconds, it was all Maddock could do to stay on his feet and keep Amalia on hers. If they stumbled, they would be trampled. But as they cleared the float, the crowd dispersed, allowing them a little more freedom of movement, and a little more speed.

A glance back showed Tiny still in pursuit, his head bobbing as he searched for them. For the moment, the crowd was still providing cover, but it was only a matter of time before the big man spotted them.

Maddock looked forward and saw a dark side street. Wooden barricades prevented vehicle access, but it looked to Maddock as if the pedestrians were also avoiding it. Probably a dead-end, but reasoning that it might give them a place to hide, Maddock steered Amalia toward it.

"Down there. Come on."

He ducked under the barricades and headed into the shadowy narrow lane beyond. To his surprise, the short street did have an outlet, but the far end was also blocked, only instead of wooden barricades, the barrier was a sleek black limousine, parked diagonally across the pavement.

They were halfway down the street before the alarm bells started ringing in Maddock's head. The presence of a limousine at a public event wasn't that unusual, but why was it blocking the street?

As a SEAL, Maddock had learned to trust his instincts. His commanding officer and surrogate father figure, Hartford "Maxie" Maxwell had drilled it into him: *If something doesn't feel right, it probably isn't.*

He stopped.

"What's wrong?" Amalia asked.

"Don't know," he said, speaking honestly. "Let's find another way."

But as he turned, he saw a pair of familiar looking characters standing just beyond the barricades behind them. Decker and Tiny regarded them across the distance, as if observing fish in the proverbial barrel.

"Okay," Maddock said slowly. "Maybe not."

The alarm bells were sounding even louder now. This *was* a trap, and they had walked right into it.

Still, if they could make it past the limo—

The doors of the black car swung open, disgorging several men. Despite their formal attire—impeccable black suits—they radiated a menace that made Decker and Tiny seem like mere pretenders. As if to confirm this impression, the men began drawing pistols from shoulder holsters concealed beneath their jackets.

Maddock skidded to a halt and reversed again. *Better to go with the devil you know,* he thought. He remained confident that Decker at least, lacked the stones for cold-blooded murder.

But the looter seemed willing to challenge that notion. As Maddock started toward the barricade, Decker and his hulking sidekick drew their pistols and aimed them at Maddock.

"Sorry, Maddock. Looks like the party's over."

Maddock couldn't help but groan. "Really?"

Decker shrugged. "What? It's perfect."

"It's cliché."

Beside him, Amalia gasped. "*Senhor* Maddock!"

"Call me Dane," he said, turning to see what had prompted her outburst. She was looking back at the limousine, and when he followed her gaze, he saw another figure emerging from the car. The elderly white-haired man was also wearing a black suit, but the cut of the garment was distinctive.

"A priest?"

Amalia shook her head, miserably. "Not a priest. This is Cardinal Sergio Ribeiro, Archbishop of Rio de Janeiro."

SEVEN

Maddock and Amalia were hustled down the length of the street to stand before the cardinal. The latter's eyes, dark and intense, were fixed on the bag Maddock still carried, a look of anticipation sparkling there. "Is that it?" he asked, almost breathless. "The reliquary?"

As he unshouldered the bag and passed it over, Maddock exchanged a glance with Amalia. "How did he know what it was?"

"It's my fault," Amalia whispered. "I contacted the diocese, hoping to learn the history of the reliquary."

"Do not trouble yourself with regret, my child," the cardinal said, the ghost of a smile playing across his lined face. "Your call only confirmed what I already suspected. The mask and the reliquary were lost together. It only stood to reason that they would be found together as well."

"So, you know what it is?" Maddock pressed, curious despite himself.

Ribeiro did not answer, but lowered the heavy burden to the ground, and knelt before it with what almost passed for reverence. He opened the bag, exposing the reliquary, and then without pause, rolled the chest over so that the doors were facing skyward, and opened them.

A sigh escaped his lips. "*É exatamente como Nóbrega descreveu,*" he whispered.

Maddock worked out a rough translation. *Exactly like Nóbrega described. But who's Nóbrega?*

He glanced at Amalia again, and saw a look of

recognition. She knew the answer to that question, but the cardinal clearly knew a lot more than any of them.

"If you knew what we had," Maddock said, "why go to all the trouble of having those morons—" He jerked a thumb toward Decker and Tiny. "—steal it from us?"

"*Sim*," Amalia added. "I would have given it to you if you had only asked. In fact, that was our intention all along. Anything we discovered would have been a gift to the people of Brazil. Holy relics are already the property of the Church. Obviously, we would have gladly returned them to you."

Ribeiro looked up, seeming to consider the question. His eyes flicked to Decker. "Perhaps that would have been the wiser course. *Senhor* Decker has certainly drawn more attention our way than I would have liked."

"I don't get it," Maddock said, trying to capitalize on the cleric's evident willingness to talk. "You couldn't have known... You couldn't have even suspected that I would find what I did. Yet you had Decker waiting in the wings, ready to pounce."

"Actually, I did know," the cardinal said, his smile indicating that he was all too happy to share the information. "Or rather, I knew that this was among the many forgotten treasures that litter the floor of Guanabara Bay. But to answer your question, I was simply covering my bets. You see, I do not like surprises. Whether you found Roman artifacts or buried treasure... Or nothing at all, it was imperative that I know before anyone else. To spare the Church any embarrassment. He—" Another scathing glance at Decker. "—was instructed merely to observe you without interfering, which he assured me he could do. Your discovery of the Nóbrega artifacts was serendipitous, as was his subsequent intervention."

There was that name again. Nóbrega.

"A native mask and an empty reliquary?" Maddock pressed, hoping to prompt the cardinal into revealing something, without sounding too eager. "Seems like you're missing something. Like maybe a relic to go in the reliquary?"

The older man smiled, his snow-white eyebrows twitched. "That is nothing that need concern you. In fact, I think I have already said enough." He closed the reliquary and then, with some effort, lifted the bag and placed it inside the waiting limousine. He then turned to Decker again. "Kill them."

He said it with such dispassion that, for a moment Maddock thought he had misheard. Evidently, so did Decker. "Excuse me?"

"Did I stutter? You've made a mess of this. Now it's time to take responsibility."

Amalia let out a gasp, as if only now comprehending the cardinal's original pronouncement. "Kill us?"

"I'm not a killer," Decker protested. "You've got what you want. And like she said, it belongs to you anyway. No harm, no foul."

The cardinal's eyes drew into venomous slits. "No harm?" He hissed. "They know of my involvement, thanks to your incompetence."

"Then you do it," Decker said, taking a step back. "I don't want any part of a murder."

"Don't you get it, Decker?" Maddock said. "You're the fall guy."

"Fall guy?" Tiny echoed, his face contorted with confusion. "Fall? I forget the seasons are different down here."

Maddock and the others ignored him.

"He's already written the script, and you're perfect for the part," he continued to Decker. "Everyone knows what a crook you are, so nobody will question the narrative."

"What narrative?" Decker asked.

"You kill us after stealing the relic, and then his men kill you in self-defense. No loose ends."

Decker's eyes widened, and then his attention snapped back to the cardinal, along with the aimpoint of his pistol. It was only then that he realized that Ribeiro's bodyguards already had their weapons aimed at him and his sidekick. "Whoa!" he shouted, quickly redirecting the weapon skyward, both arms raised in a show of non-aggression. "Hold on. That wasn't our deal."

Ribeiro did not answer the challenge directly, but instead turned to the nearest of his bodyguards—a walking mountain of a man who seemed about to burst the seams of his black suit. "Hugo. *Mate todos.*" Then, he climbed into the limousine, closing the door firmly behind him.

Without turning his head to look at her, Maddock squeezed Amalia's hand to get her attention and whispered. "Get ready to move." Then, he addressed Decker. "Tough luck," he remarked.

"I won't do it," Decker muttered, letting his gun fall. It hit the pavement with a dull metallic clank. "Can't pin nothing on me if I don't pull the trigger."

"The police will believe whatever he tells them. And you don't have to be alive to pull a trigger."

Decker looked down at his pistol in dismay. "Crap, you're right."

Maddock could see indecision in the other man's

eyes, in his body language. Decker was going to go for the gun, he had no choice, but the moment he tried, Ribeiro's men would open fire. They wouldn't be aiming for Maddock or Amalia, as that wouldn't support the fictional narrative, but that was no guarantee of safety once the shooting started. Maddock squeezed Amalia's hand again, signaling her that he was about to make his move.

Suddenly, the shadowy lane was filled with light and music. Maddock turned, along with everyone else, to the source of the disturbance behind them, just as the lumbering parade float they had passed earlier crashed through the barricades and began rolling like a juggernaut down the empty street.

"*Me Deus*," Amalia gasped.

"Not quite," Maddock said, grinning. "Come on." Without letting go of her hand he started down the street at a brisk run. A moment later, the shooting started.

Maddock thrust Amalia ahead of him, shielding her from the bullets that were pinging off pavement and the sides of the buildings that lined the street. More than a few sizzled past them, striking the float in a series of eruptions that looked like confetti poppers exploding. Thankfully, the ponderous mobile platform appeared to have already been abandoned by the samba performers they had seen earlier.

The float itself was too wide for the narrow street, but that didn't seem to matter to its unseen operator. It kept advancing, the metal frame underneath the decorations scraping against the buildings to either side in a shower of friction sparks. Maddock doubted it would be able to go much further, but suspected the driver's real intent was simply to provide a diversion, allowing Amalia and him to escape, and to block the street to prevent the killers from pursuing. Unfortunately, it had done too good a job of the latter. There was no way to get around the float; they would have to either climb over it or….

Maddock pointed to the narrow space between the bottom of the overhanging platform and the pavement. "Down. We'll have to crawl for it."

More bullets smacked into the float, throwing up bits of brightly colored debris that rained down on them even as they slid underneath it and started belly crawling down its length.

Like the brightly-colored plumage of a tropical bird, the float's exterior covering concealed a truly bizarre-looking creature. From below, Maddock could see its skeleton—a complicated arrangement of metal beams welded together to distribute the weight of the cantilevered platform, creating the illusion that it was hovering above the ground—and the skin of chicken wire and fiberglass that covered it. The big hollow shell acted like a sounding board, amplifying the music and the bullet impacts to almost deafening volume.

At the center of the contraption was the stripped-down chassis of a large truck—the sole means of locomotion for the prodigious contraption—and crammed into the low-slung control cockpit was their grinning savior.

"Like my new ride?" Bones had to shout to be heard over the din. "It handles like an aircraft carrier, but it's pimped out. Gotta love all the accessories!"

"Accessories?" Amalia asked, her curiosity momentarily overpowering her survival instincts.

"I think he means the dancers," Maddock explained.

"Exotic dancers," Bones confirmed with a lascivious grin.

"Hate to break it to you, but I think they all fell off."

Bones face fell, but then he shrugged and slipped out of the seat to join them. "Screw it. It was just a test drive. I wasn't planning to keep it."

Maddock expected to emerge into a scene of total pandemonium, but instead, they found the street practically deserted. Most of the spectators and performers had fled the chaos. Only a few small clusters of people remained, some of them evidently nursing injuries sustained in the stampede.

"You see Matt anywhere?" he asked Bones.

"Last I saw him, he was limping off the field. Rico Suave was helping him. He'll be all right."

Maddock didn't like the idea of abandoning his crewmate to an uncertain fate, but he knew Bones was right. "We need to find somewhere to hole up."

"Not the boat?"

Maddock shook his head. "Probably not a good idea. That's the first place he'll look for us. In fact, we should call Willis. Have him head out to sea for a while." He turned to Amalia. "You know somewhere we can go? Somewhere where he won't be able to find us?"

Amalia looked thoughtful for a moment, then nodded. "Yes, I know a place."

"You're not talking about Decker, are you?" Bones said, and then gave him a sidelong glance. "You lost it, didn't you?"

"Long story. I'll tell you all about it. But if that thing is what I think it is, we've got bigger problems than Decker."

EIGHT

"Nice place," Bones remarked, making little effort to hide his sarcasm as he allowed his gaze to drift up and down the mostly deserted street. "I guess they don't do Carnaval up here."

"Street" was actually a generous term for the irregular dirt road, lined on either side with ramshackle multi-story buildings, most of which appeared to have been fashioned out of scrap wood and cast-off signs, and looked like they might fall down in a stiff breeze. There were no street lights or traffic signals here—not much in the way of vehicle traffic, either—but if the dangerous looking tangle of insulated cables suspended from weathered wooden posts, shooting out in every direction like spider-webs was any indication, there was electricity at least part of the time. The sun had sunk deep into the western sky, casting long shadows, which were only heightened by the near total absence of artificial light.

"Actually," Amalia countered, "they do. Or rather, they go down the hill to join the festival. Many of the finest samba performers and musicians are from the *favelas*. I think sometimes that, having nothing, the poor and disenfranchised find better ways to express themselves—through art and music—than *os residentes de asfalto*."

Asfalto—asphalt—was, Maddock had learned, the local term for the developed parts of Rio de Janeiro—the "official" city—and the more affluent people who inhabited it. But nearly a quarter of the people inhabiting the greater metropolitan area lived "*na Colina*"—"on the hill"—in makeshift, unplanned, neighborhoods which had, over the last half-century, grown almost organically on the undeveloped hillsides above the city proper.

Maddock knew all about the infamous favelas. The shantytowns, which had been featured in numerous movies and video games, were reputedly lawless, violent slums, ruled by criminal gangs and drug traffickers, so he was both surprised and alarmed when Amalia led them across the bridge from Fundão Island, and then turned south, leaving the pavement behind to make the gentle climb up the primitive dirt paths of the Maré neighborhood.

Maddock felt as if he had just stepped into a war zone, and the eerily deserted streets only intensified his anxiety. He kept his head on a swivel, maintaining 360 degrees of awareness, sometimes glimpsing movement at the edge of his vision, figures retreating into the shadows, darting under ragged curtains across windows and doorways.

He strove to project an aura of danger with his body language. That, and hand-to-hand fighting skills would be their only defense if they ran afoul of hostile locals. He could see Bones doing the same, but Amalia's demeanor was different. While not exactly blasé about the environment through which they were moving, she exhibited a confidence born of familiarity.

"Here," Amalia said, making an abrupt turn down a particularly narrow, and particularly dark, alley. To Maddock, it was indistinguishable from a dozen they had already passed, but Amalia seemed to recognize where they were. Halfway down the alley's length, she mounted a rickety staircase and began ascending.

Maddock appraised the splintering wooden treads

that squeaked beneath Amalia's every step. He doubted they would hold the weight of three people, but as she reached the second-floor landing, Amalia leaned out and called down to them. "What are you waiting for? Come."

Bones shrugged and then stepped up, but as his weight settled onto his leading foot, there was a loud, torturous creaking sound.

"I've been telling him to lose weight," Maddock said in a stage whisper to Amalia, "but he likes his burgers and beer too much."

"Screw you, Maddock." Bones grimaced, but then took another step, and another. Miraculously, the structure held together, but Maddock waited until Bones cleared the first flight before following.

He caught up to Bones and Amalia on the third floor, standing before a curtained doorway. As he approached them, Amalia leaned close to the curtain and called out softly. "Ana! It's Amalia. I am here with two friends. May we come in?"

A moment later, the curtain parted a couple inches, but the interior of the dwelling remained too dark for him to make out the occupant. "Amalia?" asked a female voice. "Who is that with you?"

"Dane Maddock and, uh, Bones Breaksomething."

A sound that might have been a chuckle issued from behind the curtain. "Tourists, Amalia?"

Amalia shook her head. "Nothing like that. Please, let us in. We have much to discuss."

There was a long pause, then a sigh. "Very well." The curtain drew back and Amalia strode forward into the dark interior. As soon as Maddock and Bones were inside, the curtain was replaced, and then a battery powered lantern blazed to life, revealing a small room with a worn but serviceable futon couch, a similarly distressed chair and a coffee table. Resting on the latter was a laptop computer—closed—and a mug filled with a steaming beverage. Their host placed the lantern on the tabletop, and gestured for them all to sit.

"This is Ana Coelho," Amalia said simply.

Ana Coelho looked to be in her late twenties, tall and willowy, with long straight black hair and an olive complexion. She was pretty, but in an understated way, unlike Amalia. Her faded T-shirt and ragged denim jeans seemed to Maddock like camouflage. A way to blend in with the locals. Ana did not strike him as someone who belonged in the favela.

As Amalia completed the introductions, he learned that this assessment was only partly correct. "Ana is a journalist," she explained. "She writes about the favelas."

"So, you don't actually live here," Bones said, making no effort to hide his relief at this apparent revelation. "This is just an assignment."

Ana arched an eyebrow. "As a matter of fact, I do live here," she said. Her accent was not as heavy as Amalia's, and her sharp tone held more than a hint of indignation. "I grew up here. This is not an assignment. It is my… my passion. I tell the stories of the people who live in places like these. The real stories. Not the lies the government wants you to believe."

"Lies?" Maddock asked.

"That we are all criminals," Ana snapped. "That gangs rule the favelas."

"But it is a problem, isn't it?"

"They want to dehumanize us. Tear down what we have accomplished here, what we have built for ourselves without their help. They deny us basic human rights, and then when it pleases them, they send in their shock troops to *pacify* us."

Maddock thought she sounded more like an activist than a journalist, but he took her point. There were always two sides to every story. Sometimes, more.

Ana thrust her chin toward him in a dismissive gesture, then returned her attention to Amalia. "Why have you brought them here?"

"Someone tried to kill us, Ana."

"I'm not surprised. You should have telephoned me. I would have come to you."

"No, Ana, you don't understand." She quickly related everything that had happened—from Maddock's discovery to their narrow escape from Cardinal Ribeiro's goons. As she told the story, Ana's indignant expression faded, to be replaced by real concern.

"Ribeiro? The cardinal wants you dead?" Ana said, eyes wide with disbelief.

"That's only part of it," Maddock said, leaning forward. "He's got something planned for that reliquary. Something very bad."

"Like what?" Ana pressed.

Maddock wasn't quite ready to share his thoughts on what Ribeiro might be planning, not because he didn't trust the others, but because he couldn't quite bring himself to believe the crazy theory. "Tell me about the cardinal. What kind of man is he?"

Ana gave a derisive snort. "That *filho da puta*? He is no friend of the people."

"Why do you say that?"

Amalia fielded the question. "Are you familiar with the modern history of my country?"

Maddock sensed it was a rhetorical question, and so

simply shook his head, prompting her to make her point.

"The Brazilian Church has always been very progressive, particularly with respect to ministering to the poor. Part of this, I am sure, is due to the strong influence of the Jesuit order, going back to the early colonial period. After the military coup in 1964, the Church leadership took a more active role in providing for the people, especially the poor and the indigenous peoples. Many parish priests were advocates of Liberation Theology, offering protection and support to political enemies of the government. But not everyone in the Church agreed with that position."

"I take it Cardinal Ribeiro fell into the latter camp."

"*Father* Ribeiro was a traditionalist who openly opposed the philosophy of Liberation Theology, equating it with Marxism, and therefore, with godlessness. Like many young men, he was a zealot. While that did not make him many friends among the people of Brazil, it did gain him allies among the more conservative figures in the Church hierarchy."

"Time and experience has not softened him," added Ana. "He opposes any reforms, even those that might ease human suffering. He spoke out against the Pope... The Pope! Can you believe it? During the Zika outbreak a couple years ago, he accused the Pope of bowing to liberal pressure over the question of using birth control. Ribeiro believes the pontiff is a dangerous liberal reformer with a secret secular agenda. He even claims that the Pope's election was illegitimate, since his predecessor still lives. He despises the Pope, and makes no secret of it.

"Would that be the same Pope who's dropping by tomorrow?" Bones asked, innocently.

Amalia nodded, then her head snapped around to face Maddock. "You don't think…?"

Maddock stroked his chin. "I think the timing is suspicious."

Ana's eyes darted from Maddock to Amalia, then back again. "You think Cardinal Ribeiro could be plotting against the Holy Father?"

"Would it surprise you if it's true?"

Ana's shrug was answer enough.

"But what about the reliquary?" Amalia asked. "How is that important to his plan?"

"I'm still trying to figure that out," Maddock admitted. "Ribeiro said something earlier. A name. Norbega?"

Bones snapped his fingers. "That's the 'Mambo Number Five' dude, right?" He started gyrating his shoulders and crooning. "A little bit of Ana in my life. A little bit Amalia by my side—"

"Bones! Shut it!"

"That was Lou Bega," Ana sighed, rolling her eyes. "*Idiota*."

Bones grinned. "That's Brazilian for sex god, right?"

"Nóbrega," corrected Amalia. "He said 'Nóbrega.'"

"Does that mean anything to you?"

Both women nodded, but Amalia spoke first. "Father Manuel da Nóbrega was a Jesuit, one of the first in Brazil. He is quite famous. But I have never heard anyone speak of artifacts associated with him."

Maddock leaned back in his seat, eyes raised to the ceiling in thought. "Ribeiro knew about the mask *and* the reliquary. Maybe there's something in the historical record. Something that isn't common knowledge."

"We could Google it," Bones suggested.

Maddock laughed at the preposterous idea, but to his surprise, Ana reached out to the laptop on the table and opened it, entering her password at the prompt.

"You get WiFi here?"

"After a fashion," Ana replied, the corners of her mouth twitching into a grin. "We're very resourceful on the hill."

"Would you… Uh, mind if I used that for a second?"

Ana gave him a perturbed frown but relented, sliding the laptop over to him. Maddock quickly logged into his Skype account, selected a name from his contact list, and placed a voice call. The quiet room was suddenly filled with electronically generated ringing sounds, and then a nasally voice issued from the speaker.

"Maddock. What a surprise? How did you know I'm running low on bourbon?"

"Just had a feeling, Jimmy."

Jimmy Letson was an investigative journalist, currently working for the Washington Post, but in an earlier life, he and Maddock had started SEAL training together. Jimmy had washed out early on, but they had remained friends. Maddock frequently made use of Jimmy's prodigious skills as a data retrieval specialist—in common parlance, a hacker—to run down obscure leads, paying for services rendered with large quantities of Wild Turkey bourbon whiskey.

"I need you to look something up for me," Maddock went on.

"No? Really?" Jimmy laughed. "I would complain that, with you, it's never a social call, but you're boring as hell, so I prefer it this way."

Amalia and Ana exchanged grins.

"It's true," Bones mouthed.

"Guilty as charged, Maddock said. "Can you help me out?"

The skinny, curly-haired hacker grinned. "Lay it on me, brother."

"I need everything you can get on a Jesuit priest named Manuel da Nóbrega." He glanced over at Amalia to verify the pronunciation and received a nod.

"Not to be confused with Lou Bega," Bones added unnecessarily.

"You would have to be an idiot to confuse the two," Jimmy fired back. Ana shot Bones a triumphant grin.

"What about Noriega?"

"Shut your hole, Bones. I'm trying to work."

They lapsed into an anticipatory silence, with only the faint clicking of fingers on a keyboard coming through the laptop speaker. After what felt like an eternity, Jimmy spoke again.

"Father Manuel da Nóbrega. Born in 1517. Portuguese priest and a Jesuit. Went to Brazil... That the guy?"

Maddock glanced over at Amalia who nodded again. "That's him. We're looking for anything that might connect him to some relics that we found in Rio de Janeiro. Specifically, a golden mask that looks like a native headdress. And a golden reliquary."

"Which might be radioactive," Bones added.

"Radioactive?" Jimmy and Ana asked the question almost simultaneously.

"Don't worry about that right now," Maddock said quickly, though part of him wondered if that wasn't the detail on which everything hinged.

"Huh. Okay. You said Rio, right? It's Carnaval season down there, isn't it? You jerks could have invited me."

"Is it? Hadn't noticed."

"Okay, it looks like Nóbrega came to Brazil in 1549. Worked extensively with the native tribes, running interference between them and the colonists who wanted to use them as slaves. He actually thought the colonists were a bad influence on the Indians, and tried to keep them separate. Then it looks like something changed in 1559. The Bishop of Brazil, Dom Pedro Fernandes Sardinha, was killed and eaten by natives... Oh, that's weird."

"What's weird? Besides the cannibalism, I mean."

"Well, it says here that he was 'slaughtered with an apple.'"

"Bashed over the head with a laptop?" Bones mused.

"Must be some kind of glitch with the translation," Jimmy muttered. "Hold on." There was a brief pause, then Jimmy spoke again. "'*Abatido com uma maça.*' That's what it says."

Ana and Amalia exchanged a glance, then both nodded. "Yes," Ana confirmed. "That means 'slaughtered with an apple.'"

"You said they ate him, right?" Bones said. "Maybe they shoved an apple in his mouth first. You know, like a roast pig? And they probably shoved the stick in his…"

"Please don't," Ana said.

Maddock winced and tried, unsuccessfully, to banish that mental image.

"It's weird though," Jimmy went on, "Because apples aren't native to the Americas. They weren't brought over from Europe until 1607."

"Maybe 'apple' is just a placeholder for some other fruit?" Bones suggested. "What goes well with roast priest?"

"Maybe it's an allusion to the Bible, and the word apple refers to a poisonous or dangerous fruit," Amalia said. "The fruit of the cashew tree is called an apple. It contains a poisonous compound that can blister the skin, and produces toxic smoke if burned."

"Let's put the apple on the back burner for now," Maddock admonished. "You said things changed for Nóbrega after that. What happened?"

"Oh. Uh, let's see. It sounds like his attitude toward the natives changed a little. He started focusing on educating the native children. Indoctrinating them at a young age. Nothing about relics or masks. Oh, here's something. The French Huguenots tried to establish a colony in Rio—Fort Coligny—and they formed alliances with some of the native tribes to fight against the Portuguese. Nóbrega was obliged to support the Portuguese campaigns against the French and by extension, the natives who were working with them. The French were finally kicked out in 1567. That was when the city of Rio de Janeiro was founded. Nóbrega established a Jesuit college there, and ran it until he died in 1570. He actually died on his fifty-third birthday."

"Fifty-three? That's pretty young. How did he die?"

"Not finding that here, but remember where he was. Rio was a rural backwater. He was living with tropical diseases, cannibals—"

"Poison apples," added Bones.

"Those, too. And they didn't exactly worry about establishing cause of death back then. Anyway, story ends there."

Maddock shook his head. "Dig deeper, Jimmy. Those relics were on a ship that sank in Guanabara Bay.

Let's assume that Nóbrega put them aboard. Maybe there's some record of cargo? Maybe he was going to ship them back to Portugal. The ship left Rio but never made it out into open ocean. Maybe there was a storm and it got blown back into the bay where it sank."

"The reliquary was empty," Amalia said.

"But why did he send the reliquary away at all? And what does the mask have to do with anything?"

"What does any of this have to do with a plot against the Pope?" asked Ana, sounding frustrated.

"If we figure out why the reliquary is important, we'll have the answer."

"What if…" Amalia started, but then shook her head, as if the thought was not worth the effort of uttering aloud.

"Go on," Maddock prompted.

"Well, let's say that Nóbrega found these things after the French were defeated. The mask, the reliquary and something else. A native artifact."

"What kind of artifact?"

She spread her hands helplessly. "I don't know. It is a stupid idea."

"It's already better than anything I've got," Bones said.

Amalia offered him a grateful smile, but before she could go on, Jimmy let out whoop of elation. "I think I found something. It's a letter from our boy, Padre Nóbrega to Father Diego Laynez, who was the Superior General of the Jesuit order. I'll just skip to the relevant bits. And bear in mind, this is a computerized translation, so…"

He trailed off, and after a momentary pause, began reading aloud:

"'On February 20 of this year, I was summoned to the bedroom of Dom Estácio de Sá, the beloved nephew of our Governor General to pray over him and prepare his soul for passage to the next life. Dom Estácio was reported to have suffered a severe wound from an Indian arrow on the day of his victory against the French heretics and their army of savages, but when I spoke to him, he uttered a very different account of what happened during that battle. This is the tale I heard from his own lips.'"

When Jimmy paused to catch his breath, Amalia spoke. "Estácio de Sá was the leader of the Portuguese forces fighting the Huguenots, and the founder of Rio de Janeiro. He led the final attack but was hit by an arrow in the eye and died a month later, probably from an infection."

Bones winced. "It's always the eyes," he muttered.

"That's not the story he told Nóbrega," Jimmy countered. "This next part is Estácio dictating:

"'As I entered with my army into the palisade of Uruçu-mirim, I found, not a force of men fighting, for in fact, most had already perished or fled before our guns, but a Tamoyana witch. He wore a golden crown that hid his eyes and long bark-cloths woven with gold thread, and in his hands he held a stone vessel, from which glowed the devil's fire. I killed him, taking his head off with one blow of my sword. As he died, the stone vessel fell from his grip and the devil's fire went out. All that remained was a single ember—a white stone, fallen from the vessel to cool on the blood-soaked ground. I returned the stone to the vessel, intending to bear it away from that place, but as soon as I did, the devil's fire returned, so I immediately

separated them again. I did not know that the death curse of the Tamoyana witch was already upon me.'"

At the mention of "devil's fire," Maddock's pulse quickened, but he withheld comment, letting Jimmy finish.

"This next part is Nóbrega again. *'I do not know if his story is true or simply a fever dream, but I touched the white stone and felt the heat still radiating from it, even a month later. With his last breath, Dom Estácio implored me to consecrate the white stone as a sacred relic, so that its evil power might be banished from the world. Consequently, I marked the white stone with the symbol of our Society and fashioned the stone vessel into a sacred reliquary, but this was not enough to prevent devil's fire from issuing forth when the stone was placed inside the vessel. Only keeping them separate can hold the evil in abeyance. I am sending the vessel to you, along with the golden crown that Dom Estacio took from the head of the Tamoyana witch. It may be that you find the means to lift the curse where I failed.'*

"That's pretty much the end of that," Jimmy said, "But I don't think it's much of a leap to guess that the ship that was supposed to take those items back to Europe is the wreck you found. Evidently, it didn't get very far."

"The relic must have stayed with Father Nóbrega in Rio until his death," Maddock surmised.

"And after," Amalia added. "It would have remained at the Jesuit college on Morro do Castelo—Castle Hill— near where the airport is today. The Jesuits were expelled from Brazil in 1759, and the school was used as a military headquarters after that. The Jesuits returned eventually and built a new college in Botafogo. The original building was demolished in the 1920s, but the bell and some of the other trophies were returned to them. The relic must have been part of that collection. Cardinal Ribeiro might have found it and realized what it was. Maybe he also read Father Nóbrega's letter."

"Even if all that is true," Ana said, "I still don't see how any of this adds up to a plot against the Pope. Maybe the cardinal just wants to put a holy relic back in a sanctified reliquary."

"You heard what the dude said," Bones countered. "Devil's fire. It's not a holy relic. It's a cursed native artifact that will burn your eyes out if you aren't wearing the special mask."

He said it with a laugh, but Maddock knew he wasn't entirely joking.

"It really is similar to the Lead Mask Case," Amalia murmured.

Ana's eyebrows shot up in dismay. That was a part of their earlier discussion that they had not shared with her.

"The Lead Masks Case?" Jimmy said.

"You know the story?" Maddock asked.

"It's only one of the weirdest unsolved mysteries of the Twentieth Century. Does that have something to do with this?"

"Umm, we're not really sure," Maddock replied

"Okay, I'll just say what I know you're thinking," Bones said. "This relic is radioactive. The natives probably made a totem or something from a piece of uranium ore. We know that the Spanish found some of the stuff not far from here. The reliquary is shielded, so it's the only safe way to move the relic. The Cardinal has had the relic all along, and he knows what it really is. He needs the reliquary to transport the relic away from wherever he's got it hidden, so he can put it in a dirty bomb."

From his townhouse thousands of miles away, Jimmy caught the thread. "That totally works. That's probably what happened to the guys with the lead masks. They were trying to do something with the relic, but they didn't know what they were doing and died of radiation poisoning."

"Radiation doesn't kill instantly," Maddock countered. "It can take weeks, or even years, for an exposure to kill. Whatever killed them, it wasn't radiation. And if this was just about transporting radioactive materials, Ribeiro wouldn't need the reliquary. He could buy lead sheeting from a hardware store."

Amalia jumped to Bones' defense. "But the reliquary would be the perfect way to transport it if he wanted to get it close to the Pope."

Maddock sat up suddenly, inspiration dawning. "The reliquary isn't for transporting the relic," he said, still half-thinking aloud. He looked up at the others. "I know what he's going to do with it."

NINE

Cardinal Sergio Ribeiro sat alone in the dimly lit study of his private apartment staring, not at the golden reliquary or the mask—both of which sat on a side table near the door, but instead at the small wooden box which occupied the center of his desk. It was a simple cigar box, unremarkable in every way. Ribeiro could not recall where he had acquired it; he had smoked cigarettes for many years, but never cigars. In any event, the box was of little interest to him, but in its own way, it was like the jar in the old Greek myth of Pandora. If he opened it, if he revealed the secret he had kept for more than fifty years, the world would be changed forever.

But it would be a change for the better. He believed that with every fiber of his being. And so, really, what choice did he have?

Smiling, he leaned forward and flipped back the lid. Inside, resting on a yellowed piece of old newspaper, was a crude disc shape, upon which a distinctive sigil had been inscribed—a sun-circle with thirty-two rays, alternating straight and wavy points, and inside the circle were a cross, three nails, and the letters IHS—a Christogram, or representation of the name of Jesus.

It was the sigil of the Society of Jesus. The Jesuits.

The cardinal may not have recalled the origin of the cigar box, but he remembered every detail of the day he had acquired the relic.

"Bless me father, for I have sinned," came the whispered voice behind the screen.

Despite the appearance of anonymity, Father Ribeiro had no difficulty recognizing the voice of the penitent. It was Father Marques, a junior priest from a neighboring parish. Ribeiro had only met Marques a couple of times, and had taken an immediate dislike to the outspoken young man, whose sermons seemed more like the propaganda of the communist revolutionaries than the word of God.

It was a growing problem in the Church, and in South America in particular. Secularism, disguised as an appeal to social justice was insinuating even into the upper hierarchy of the Church, turning priests into revolutionaries, and bishops and cardinals into quiet blasphemers. No, it wasn't a problem, he corrected, it was war. Spiritual warfare, and nothing less than the future of the Holy Church lay in the balance.

Oh, yes, Father Marques, he thought. *You have sinned.*

Marques went on, unaware of his confessor's thoughts. "In the name of the Father, and of the Son, and of the Holy Spirit. My last confession was one week ago."

"You are not a member of this flock," Ribeiro said. It was a small breach of protocol, but a necessary one he judged. "Why do you come here to offer your confession?"

Marques swallowed nervously. "I came to you…" A pause. "I came to you because I think only you can help me."

The answer surprised Ribeiro. "Only God can help you, my son. What are your sins?"

As Marques told his story, Ribeiro's contempt for the man was supplanted in turn by astonishment and anger.

He had not been wrong about Marques. The young priest had fallen in with a group of Marxist troublemakers who were not content to merely protest the governments actions or oppose it through peaceful means. No, they meant to overthrow the government with violence. And Marques had given them the means to do so.

The relic.

The young priest had discovered the Jesuit sigil among the trophies removed from the old college in Castelo, along with letters that not only established its provenance as formerly belonging to the first Jesuit in Brazil—Father Manuel da Nóbrega—but also explaining its truly bizarre history.

It was a story of native sorcerers unleashing a terrible, unholy magic using a piece of silvery metal and a box of stone—magic with the power to cause pestilence and death. Nóbrega had tried to sanctify the unholy relic by inscribing the Jesuit symbol upon it, but had ultimately hidden it away, while fashioning the stone box into a reliquary which he had sent back to Portugal for safe-keeping. His intention, no doubt, had been to transport the relic separately, and then upon arriving, demonstrate its unnatural properties, but the ship bearing the reliquary and the strange mask worn by the native shaman, had been lost in a storm almost immediately upon embarking.

Marques, who had gone to University before going to Seminary, and who, unlike Nóbrega, had been born into the Atomic Age, recognized both the description of the effects and the metal itself.

Uranium.

That knowledge had led the young priest down the

devil's path. He shared the revelation with one of the leaders of a revolutionary group—a man he counted as a friend—and had, without even realizing it, been drawn into a plot to create a weapon. An atomic weapon.

Neither man knew the first thing about creating such a weapon, but the revolutionary believed he knew someone to do the work for them—two self-identified experts from Campos dos Goytacazes. Marques had arranged a meeting with the two men to hand over the relic, even taking the precautionary measure of instructing them to fashion lead masks and wear protective garments, similar to what Nóbrega had described, and providing iodine tablets as a prophylactic measure against exposure to radiation.

For a time, Marques had fooled himself into believing that he was God's instrument—a sword, when necessary—but as the day of the assignation drew close, his conscience got the better of him. Surely, God would not want his servants to fashion weapons of indiscriminate destruction. Yet, he was trapped. If he failed to deliver the relic to the bomb makers, his so-called friend in the revolutionary movement would learn of it, and might even threaten the Church.

"What can I do, father?" Marques had wailed.

"Do not trouble yourself, my son. I will take care of the situation. Perform an act of contrition. Go, and sin no more." He paused, and then added. "One other thing. Give me the relic."

Ribeiro had known that simply taking possession of the relic would not be the end of the matter. The two bomb-makers would also have to be dealt with, permanently. Marques had unwittingly provided him with the means to eliminate them. It had been a simple thing to replace the iodine tablets with cyanide capsules. After the two men had succumbed to the poison, he had dumped their bodies on Vintém Hill, and had taken the additional measure of planting evidence to suggest that the men were members of a mystical cult, willing to ingest poison in order to commune with spirit entities.

Subsequently, Ribeiro had learned that the two "experts" would not have possessed the technical knowledge to create an atomic weapon, and even if they had, the small amount of uranium in the relic would not have been sufficient to do so. Nevertheless, his conscience was clear. The men had been enemies of the Church... Enemies of God, and he was the sword of judgment. They had not been the last wicked men to fall under that sword. The American treasure hunters he had hired to keep an eye on Dane Maddock were only the latest enemy casualties in the war. Even now, Hugo was sailing Sam Decker's boat, bearing the bodies of its crew, out into the Atlantic, where he would scuttle the craft, erasing all trace of the foreigners. Maddock and his crew would also have to be taken care of, along with the meddlesome woman from the Global Heritage Commission.

Ribeiro did not consider these to be criminal actions. In the final accounting, the Lord would hold him blameless. The discovery of Nóbrega's reliquary on the very eve of the arrival of the greatest enemy—the false pope—could not be anything but providential.

But first, he had to know if Nóbrega's account was true.

The relic was radioactive—he had checked it with a Geiger counter shortly after obtaining it from Marques—

but its output of ionizing radiation was well below the safety threshold for incidental exposure. If his plan was going to work, he would have to unlock its full potential, just as the native shaman had done four-and-a-half centuries earlier.

He rose from his desk, leaving the relic in its paper nest in the cigar box, and crossed to the table where he had deposited the mask. He picked it up, hefting it, feeling its weight. Gold, he had learned, was an effective radiation shield, and malleable enough for even primitive natives with limited knowledge of metallurgy to shape according to their whim. He could not imagine how those savages had discovered this unique property of gold, any more than he could conceive of them unlocking the power of the atom, but what other explanation could there be for the effects Nóbrega had described.

He laid the mask aside and reached for the parcel he had acquired earlier in the day. The box was even heavier than the mask, not surprisingly since it contained a heavy lead apron designed for use in X-ray laboratories. Nóbrega's letters had described the priests wearing heavy robes of native fiber which had probably been about as effective at shielding them from radiation as the raincoats worn by the two would-be bomb makers. Ribeiro wasn't going to take any chances.

He donned the lead apron and then placed the golden mask atop his head, tilting it back so that his eyes were only partly covered. The combined weight of apron and mask was almost too much for him to bear. He could feel every ounce on his shoulders and in his knees. "Lord, give me strength," he whispered, and then started back across the room to the relic. It too, felt heavy, much heavier than he remembered.

He shuffled back over to the reliquary, and then, because he knew he could not bear the weight much longer, opened the doors and thrust the silvery-white disc inside. It occurred to him that he ought not look at it directly, so he quickly reached up and tilted the mask down to cover his eyes, but not before his saw the inside of the box come alive with pale blue light.

TEN

Maddock racked his brain, trying to dredge up the memory. It was something he had read somewhere or seen on a television documentary, but all he could recall were vague generalities. He turned back to Ana's laptop. "Jimmy, can you do a search of records from the Manhattan Project? I'm trying to remember... It was something about a scientist at Los Alamos who accidentally exposed to radiation."

Bones snapped his fingers. "Dude, that was Dr. Manhattan. From *Watchmen*. You remember? Big naked guy? Bald? Permanent case of blue balls?"

Maddock shook his head but before he could correct Bones, Jimmy had an answer. "You're talking about the Demon Core."

Maddock nodded, the name unlocking the memory he had been searching for. "That's it. There was a plutonium core that was involved in two separate fatal accidents."

"That's right," Jimmy said. "The core itself was a fourteen-pound sphere of plutonium, about three-and-a-half inches in diameter. Plutonium is pretty safe to handle under normal circumstances, but when you surround it with a material that reflects neutrons—tungsten or beryllium—those neutrons will start a self-sustaining critical fission reaction in a matter of milliseconds.

"In August of 1945, a physicist named Harry Daghlian was experimenting with creating a reflector using tungsten carbide bricks. With each brick he added, the core approached criticality. When he accidentally dropped a brick on the core, it went supercritical."

"Boom!" Bones said, dramatically.

"Actually, no. Daghlian immediately removed the brick, but he still received a lethal dose of neutron radiation and gamma radiation, and died twenty-five days later. A security guard sitting at a desk about ten feet away was also exposed, and eventually developed terminal cancer.

"Then, in May of 1946, another physicist, Louis Alexander Slotin, was performing a risky experiment using the same plutonium core and two half-spheres of beryllium, held apart with a screwdriver. Several of the senior scientists warned him that he was flirting with disaster, but he went ahead with the experiment anyway. Surprise, surprise, the screwdriver slipped and the core went instantly critical. The sphere was only in contact for about half-a-second, but that was long enough for Slotin to get a 1,000 rad dose. His body caught most of the radiation, but at least three other people in the room with him also died of cancer years later."

"Holy crap," Bones said.

Amalia stared at Maddock, wide-eyed. "That's terrible."

"After that, they started calling it 'the Demon Core,'" Jimmy concluded.

"What happened to it?" Amalia asked.

"The plan was to use it in a bomb test the following month, but the accident elevated the core's radioactive output and it took a while for it to cool down. Eventually, they melted it down and recycled it."

"You can't destroy evil just by melting it down," Bones said with a grave tone. "The Demon Core could still be out there, waiting to kill again."

Maddock ignored the ominous statement. "I think the reliquary was a primitive kind of neutron reflector. The stone box inside is probably a tungsten rich mineral."

There was a faint noise of Jimmy tapping at his keyboard. "Was it a grayish or brownish rock? With prismatic fracture planes?"

"Gray," Maddock confirmed. "You got something?"

"Wolframite. It's basically tungsten ore."

Maddock nodded. "Plutonium is almost non-existent in nature. Most of the plutonium used in nuclear weapons was produced in breeder reactors. But uranium is pretty common, and the most common form is uranium-238 which decays into plutonium-238 if you bombard it with fast neutrons. Or reflect those neutrons back by enclosing them in a tungsten matrix."

"Easy-Bake Demon Core," Bones mused.

Ana shook her head, incredulous. "You are suggesting that the indigenous people had knowledge of atomic power?"

"Is it really so crazy?" Bones retorted. He turned to Amalia as if looking for confirmation. "We barely know anything about the ancient civilizations in South America, but we do know that they had knowledge of science, math, astronomy. Is it so hard to believe that one of them might have figured out how to split the atom?"

"Frankly? Yes."

"Plus," Bones went on, undeterred, "There's a lot of evidence that aliens might have visited here. Maybe you've heard of a little thing called the Nazca Lines?"

"Two thousand miles away," scoffed Ana. "On the

other side of the Andes."

"Yeah, but a short hop by UFO."

"UFO?" Ana rolled her eyes.

Maddock intervened quickly. "I'm not saying the natives were experts in nuclear physics, but all human knowledge is the result of experimentation. Trial and error. They might have stumbled across something, even if they didn't fully understand what they had."

"So you think this relic is a radioactive core," Amalia said, "And that placing it in the reliquary will cause it to go critical, just like this Demon Core."

Maddock nodded. "And I think Cardinal Ribeiro is going to use it to try to assassinate the Pope tomorrow."

Even with everything they had uncovered, it still sounded crazy, but he pressed on. "I think he plans to present both the relic and the reliquary to the Pope. Separately, of course. He'll probably make a show of asking the Pope to bless the relic before putting it inside the chest."

"And when he does," Amalia finished, "it will release a burst of radiation."

"The symptoms won't show up for days, maybe even weeks. Even if his doctors recognize it as radiation sickness, they probably won't be able to figure out when or where the exposure occurred."

"The Holy Father is only going to be in Rio for a few hours. Just long enough to visit *Cristo Redentor*." She then clarified in English. "Christ the Redeemer."

"Then that's where he'll have to do it."

Ana's forehead creased with worry. "In the accidents with the Demon Core… You said they were only allowed to go critical for a second or two."

"If even," Jimmy replied.

She turned to Maddock. "If everything you say about this relic is true, and the cardinal does this… Tricks the Holy Father into putting this relic into the reliquary… What will happen if it is not removed right away?"

Maddock didn't know the answer, but Jimmy did. "Well, it won't go full Hiroshima if that's what you're worried about. It takes a very specific set of conditions to make that happen, and I guarantee that those natives didn't figure *that* out through trial an error. The worst-case scenario would probably be a self-sustaining nuclear reaction, but that would only last until the core melted down, which would probably happen pretty quickly."

"And radiation?"

"Oh, yeah. A lot."

Ana's gaze remained on Maddock. "Then it is not just the Holy Father that will be in danger. There will be hundreds of people up there. They will all be exposed."

"We're not going to let that happen," Maddock assured her.

"How do we stop it?" asked Bones. "Something tells me if we take this story to the police, they're more likely to lock us up than the cardinal."

Maddock couldn't disagree. "Judging by what Decker said, at least some of the police are in his pocket. And after what happened tonight, they're probably already looking for us."

"What if we contact the papal security force directly?" Amalia suggested. "Surely they would take the threat seriously."

Maddock had considered that option. "If they believe us, great. But something tells me it will be our word against Ribeiro's, and like Bones said, this is a pretty crazy story. No, I think we're going to have to do this ourselves. But that might not be as hard as it sounds. All we have to do is get either the reliquary or the relic away from the cardinal. Without both, his plan is a bust."

"The cardinal has his own security force," Amalia countered. "Getting close to him won't be easy."

"Try impossible," Ana put in.

"Well, at least we know where it's going to happen."

"Looks like we're crashing another party," Bones said with a wry grin.

Amalia shook her head. "There are only three ways to get to the top of Monte Cristo—the train, minibus, or the footpath—and the police will be guarding all of them tomorrow. We'll never get past them."

Maddock closed his eyes for a moment, trying to visualize the mountain with its iconic statue rising high above the city, just as he had seen it when *Sea Foam* cruised into Guanabara Bay a few days earlier. One memory triggered another, and inspiration dawned. "There's another way to get to the top."

ELEVEN

It had been many years since Cardinal Sergio Ribeiro last visited the summit of Corcovado mountain—known to the locals as Monte Cristo—and even longer since he recalled being impressed by either the summit, with its commanding view of the city, or the towering art deco likeness of the Savior with his arms spread wide, rising from its crown. Despite its apparent divine association, and yes, even its consecration as a holy site by one of his predecessors, Ribeiro could not think of it as anything but a symbol of all that had gone wrong in the Church, and indeed, with the whole world.

The mountaintop had become a mere tourist attraction, overrun daily with hordes of visitors, many of whom did not even profess faith in the Savior as they posed for photographs before his likeness, and bought T-shirts and coffee mugs emblazoned with images of the iconic monument. The statue itself had been co-opted as a secular symbol, an embodiment of world peace, yet without any regard for the sacrifice or teachings of the Christ.

It was, Ribeiro decided, only fitting that the false pope should want to pay it a visit. What better symbol of his campaign to gut the Church of anything remotely resembling devotion to God and scripture.

Ribeiro, accompanied by his hulking chief bodyguard Hugo, who bore the gold reliquary in his massive hands, had arrived well in advance of the VIP party, traveling up the mountain on the cog-wheel train, which utilized a special rack and pinion gear system, not unlike that used by roller coasters, to overcome the steep grade. Rather than wait in the shelter of the elevator lobby or the café, which was already overflowing with visitors, Ribeiro chose to await the arrival of his sworn enemy on the uppermost balcony, at the base of the statue itself. The morning air was chilly, the constant wind intensifying the effect, but the cardinal felt warmth radiating like divine energy from the relic tucked under his fascia—the bright red sash that was the symbol of his office.

It would not be long now. Soon, he would end the tenure of the false pope and save the Church from the cancer that was devouring it, even at the cost of his own life.

From his vantage he surveyed the crowd below and felt a swell of contempt for them. Many were members of the clergy who, despite surely knowing the peril he represented, were eager to catch a glimpse of him or take his picture, as they might a movie star or a famous *futebol* player. Fitting, he supposed, since this pope was more a celebrity than a shepherd of Christ's true flock. Indeed, he was more beloved by atheists than believers, embracing scientific progress over doctrine, casting aside centuries of tradition to demand that the Church accept and even sanctify perverted "modern" lifestyles. Ribeiro was not alone in his belief that something had to be done, and swiftly. If the false pope was not removed, the Church would be broken beyond all hope of repair.

A few of the spectators acknowledged him, but most were gazing down the hillside, watching as the papal motorcade slithered up the meandering switchbacks. A dozen police motorcycles, their lights flashing, formed the head of the column, with several police cars and unmarked SUVs following. One of the latter held the object of Ribeiro's antipathy. The narrow confines of the mountain road had precluded use of the "popemobile"— the designation for any vehicle designed to convey the pontiff in a manner that allowed him to be viewed and adored by the masses—but the man himself was visible, framed in the open window of his vehicle, leaning out and waving to the adoring crowd assembled on the fringes of the parking area at the top of the hill. Unlike his modern predecessors, this pope refused many of the defensive measures recommended by his Swiss Guard protectors, claiming that such safeguards would only create a sense of separation between himself and his flock.

Ribeiro's lips curled contemptuously at the display of mock humility. Even in this, the illegitimate pontiff insulted both the Church and his high office, subtly insinuating that he was somehow superior to all who had gone before.

As the procession reached the top of the hill, it coiled sinuously around, repositioning for ease of departure, and then doors began opening, disgorging men in black suits, who immediately clustered around their white-clad charge as he got out. The entourage disappeared from view briefly as they entered the elevator station, then reappeared on the lower landing leading to the first of two escalators designed to expedite movement to the top. The route had been cleared in advance of the pontiff's arrival, a long strip of red carpet laid out to delineate the path he would travel, but the pedestrian route—a series of short concrete stairways that ascended around the opposite side of the monument—was overflowing with well-wishers, waving and crying out to the Holy Father, who in turn waved and made gestures of benediction as he stepped onto the metal treads and began ascending.

Ribeiro knew he ought to go down and greet the pontiff, if only to maintain the illusion of respect, but could not bring himself to do so. Neither the pope nor any of the other clergy, seemed aware of his effrontery. They were all too caught up in the moment.

The cardinal felt his heart beating faster as his enemy transitioned to the second automated staircase and began rising toward the balcony. It would not be long now.

"Lord, give me strength," he whispered.

A moment later, the smiling, white-robed figure stepped off the escalator. His gaze drifted for a moment until it fixed on Ribeiro.

"*Cardeal,*" the Pope said, greeting him in Portuguese. "*É tão bom vê-lo novamente.*" He spread his arms wide, as if in imitation of the statue looming over them both, and began moving directly toward Ribeiro.

There was a knowing gleam in the pontiff's eyes. Ribeiro's contempt for the leader of the Church was well-documented, and both men knew their exchange would be watched closely by the rest of the world. If Ribeiro was anything but civil, he would face intense criticism, but if he appeared too eager to embrace the man he had called "illegitimate," those same critics would brand him a hypocrite.

Of course, none of that would matter in a few days.

Managing a smile of his own, Ribeiro opened his arms and stepped in close, accepting the other man's embrace. "*Bem-vindo ao Rio de Janeiro, Santo Padre.*"

It was all that could be expected of him. The pontiff

had not come to visit him, and nothing more was required, but Ribeiro also knew that if he did not act immediately, his opportunity to do so might slip away. The Pope's attention had already left him, his gaze moving to the other clergymen assembled nearby, and it would be only a matter of seconds before his body followed.

"Holy Father," he said, speaking quickly, a little too quickly. "I have a gift for you."

The Pope's attention swung back to him. "A gift?" His tone added what he did not voice aloud. *From you?*

Ribeiro's smile broadened. "Archaeologists working in Guanabara Bay recently discovered a holy relic that dates back to the founding of our great city." He dipped a hand under his fascia and brought forth the red velvet pouch into which he had placed the relic. He shook it out onto his palm, turning it over so that the Jesuit sigil was prominently displayed. "This belonged to Father Manuel da Nóbrega, first Provincial of the Society of Jesus in Brazil."

The Pope regarded the relic with wary curiosity. "A fascinating discovery. But this is not something you should give to me. It belongs to the Church, and the people of Brazil."

Ribeiro inclined his head. "Of course, Holy Father. But it would please me if you would bless the relic, and place it within this vessel."

He gestured toward Hugo, who immediately took a step forward, extending the golden reliquary toward the pontiff. Its doors were already open, invitingly.

The Pope's head tilted to the side for a moment, but then his smile widened as he reached out to take hold of the relic. "It would please me as well, Cardinal."

Ribeiro could barely hear the words over the rush of blood in his ears. It was done. Now he needed only stand back and allow it to happen. There would be no pain. Just a flash of blue light and an accompanying burst of heat. He would act surprised, and quickly removed the relic from the reliquary, claiming ignorance, or perhaps even declaring it a miracle. The radiation would kill him in a matter of days or perhaps mere hours, as surely as it would his enemy, but that would be a small sacrifice to save the Church.

The Pope abruptly drew back his hand as if he'd been shocked.

Ribeiro looked up in surprise and dismay. What was happening? Had his enemy sensed the danger?

Shouts of alarm cut through the noise inside his head, not just one but many voices, crying out with warnings of imminent danger and a threat to the Holy Father.

Fear gripped Ribeiro. Somehow, he had been found out, his plot discovered. But how? No one, not even Hugo, knew what he intended to do, or of the relics' deadly potential.

He stood there, frozen in place, only peripherally aware of the Swiss Guardsmen closing in around the Pope, hustling him away. He knew they would fall upon him next.

Would they arrest him? Shoot him? Or would they leave him to the mercy of the crowd? He imagined the mob seizing him, hurling him from the mountaintop.

But as the seconds ticked by and the shouts grew louder, he realized none of those dire eventualities were in the offing. Whatever was happening had nothing to do with him. The source of the threat to the pope was something else... Someone else.

Of all the damnable luck, he thought, searching the crowd for some indication of where this new danger was coming from. There was no sense of panic from the gathering, but something more like confusion, even astonishment. He followed their gazes and their pointing fingers, and realized that they were looking out, away from the mountain. A moment later, the object of their attention came into view.

A paraglider. No, two of them, swooping out from around the other side of the statue's base.

Part-parachute, part-kite, the brightly colored fabric wings were a common sight above the bay. Ribeiro knew very little about the mechanics of the contraptions, but on the occasions that he had watched them, he had always marveled at how they seemed able to stay aloft indefinitely, rising on invisible air currents, just like eagles. Evidently, the two daredevils had found a way to gain the three thousand feet of elevation required to soar around Corvocado Mountain, intent on getting as close to the summit as they could, not realizing that the Swiss Guard would immediately interpret such an action as a potential threat to the Pope.

The Pope!

He whirled around, searching for his enemy. Despite the fact that the flyers had not shown any indication of actual aggression, the Swiss Guard were hustling the pontiff away, seeking the relative safety of the limousine.

Cardinal Ribeiro felt his one chance slipping away. He had to do something.

Even without knowing what, he started forward, racing after the Swiss Guard contingent as fast as his old legs would carry him. As he moved, he called out to

Hugo, urging him to follow. He had to get the Pope to stand still long enough for him to put the radioactive disc into the stone vessel… Just a second or two would suffice, but only if he could get close enough.

With a loud rustling noise, one of the paragliders swooped down right in front of him. The suddenness of it caught Ribeiro completely by surprise, but not Hugo. In the instant before the flyer collided with him, the giant bodyguard leaped in front of him and swatted the man away with one massive arm—the reliquary safely tucked under the other. In that moment, Ribeiro caught a glimpse of the face of the man operating the glider and gasped in disbelief.

It was Dane Maddock.

TWELVE

The force of the blow spun Maddock around, but suspended as he was under the paraglider wing, he simply swung away like a pendulum until the wind caught the canopy and pulled him back into the sky. He resisted the impulse to pull on the "brakes"—the left and right toggles that were the primary means of steering the airfoil—and instead simply let the breeze carry him up and away for a few seconds in order to regain some of the momentum he had lost.

He tugged on the left brake, curling back toward the mountaintop, while straightening his legs to push the speed-bar forward, maximizing the assist from the wind. A dark shadow fell upon him as the upright cruciform figure of Christ the Redeemer came between him and the sun, and then just as quickly he was back in the light, corkscrewing up around the statue, gaining altitude as he turned into the wind. A massive outstretched arm loomed ahead and then he was under it, the flat hand nearly snagging the nylon wing as he spiraled out from beneath it, curling around to the front of the statue.

Maddock suddenly found himself gazing up into the Christ's serene visage. The glistening soapstone exterior was radiant in the direct sunlight, almost blindingly so, forcing Maddock to look away until he was past. His inadvertent glimpse had left bright green streaks across his vision, but he blinked them away just in time to see the statue's left arm right in front of him.

"Crap!" He quickly raised both toggles, letting the wing fully inflate. The wing straightened and gained both speed and elevation….

But not quite enough.

Maddock crunched his abdomen in a sloppy version of the yoga exercise known as "boat pose," lifting his extended legs as high as he dared while maintaining pressure against the speed bar, and passed over the top of the statue's arm, missing it by mere inches.

He blew out his breath in a sigh of relief, and then glanced over at the thirteen-foot-high head passing to his left. "Don't know if you had anything to do with that," he muttered, "but thanks."

Bones' voice crackled from the earpiece of his helmet's built-in radio. "Maddock, you all right?"

Maddock craned his head around and found his friend, fifty feet away on his right side, hanging under his own crescent-shaped airfoil. "I'm okay," he shouted into the voice-activated lip mic. "Cut that one a little closer than planned."

"You know, Notre Dame has Touchdown Jesus. This dude could be Incomplete Pass Jesus but his palms are facing the wrong way. Maybe we could call him WTF Jesus? Think the Brazilians would go for that?"

"If you're done blaspheming," Maddock said, "we've got work to do."

Maddock brought his gaze back to the hillside, a hundred-and-fifty-feet below. The Pope's black-suited Swiss Guard protectors were hastening their charge down the first of two long escalators, but two more dark-clad figures were right behind them—Ribeiro, easily identifiable with his scarlet sash, and the walking mountain that had swatted Maddock away like a gnat.

His name is Hugo, Maddock thought, recalling the cardinal ordering the big man to kill them all the previous night. Presumably, that death warrant was still in effect.

When he had suggested his plan the night before at Ana's little flat in the favela, Maddock had expressed the hope that he and Bones might be able to disrupt the assassination attempt simply by showing up in the sky above the mountain, but he had also known that, as long as Ribeiro possessed both the relic and the reliquary, the threat would remain.

"Looks like we're going to have to do this the hard way," Maddock said.

"I thought we already were," Bones retorted. "Or is human kite-fighting three-thousand feet above the ground your idea of easy?"

"I don't recall you voicing any objections last night. In fact, I think when I suggested it, your exact words were, 'Hells, yeah!'"

"There were chicks present. I didn't want to sound like a wuss."

Maddock laughed.

Bones' enthusiasm for the idea of paragliding to the summit of Corcovado had not been macho posturing. As seasoned skydivers, with experience using ram-air parachutes similar in most respects to paraglide airfoils, they were intimately familiar with both the risks and joys of unpowered flight.

The biggest problem had been procuring the necessary equipment on short notice, but with a little help from Jimmy, they had used social media to track down the operator of a local adventure tour company, who had accommodated their request for a paraglide tour of Tijuca Forest—which was enough to get them to their desired jumping off point—the summit of Pico da

Tijuca, about a mile due west of Corcovado. The tour company operator had been understandably upset when they had revealed their true intentions, and even more so when they left him hog-tied in his van, but Maddock felt certain he would eventually come to appreciate his small but pivotal role in their effort to save the Pope. Provided, of course, they succeeded.

Even though they could see their destination, they could not simply glide across the intervening distance. The summit of Corcovado was almost exactly the same height as their launch site, meaning they would first have to gain altitude, which necessitated a beautiful but complex aerial ballet, riding thermals—invisible columns of heated air rising from the ground below.

For the next two hours, they rose and fell, tacking like sailboats in three-dimensional space above the sprawling landscape. If not for the urgency of their mission, Maddock would have been content to spend the whole day aloft. The paraglide rigs were designed for extended periods of flight. The storage backpack, which contained an emergency reserve chute, served double-duty as a rather comfortable hammock chair.

They had climbed to an altitude of nearly eight thousand feet—high enough that they would be nearly indistinguishable to anyone on the mountaintop—and stayed there, turning lazy circles while they waited for updates from Amalia and Ana; the latter had used her press credentials to gain access to the summit of Corcovado and had kept a close watch on Cardinal Ribeiro. When the motorcade bearing the distinguished visitor finally stopped, Maddock and Bones had executed a maneuver known as a "spiral dive"—which pretty much was exactly what it sounded like—and corkscrewed down toward their destination in a flurry of noise and motion that had not gone unnoticed by the crowd gathered near the summit.

That, Maddock had known, had been the riskiest part of the plan. The Pope might have been a man of peace, but his protectors—the Swiss Guard—were seasoned military veterans, armed to the teeth, and ready to kill-or-be-killed in defense of the Holy Father. If they felt the situation warranted it, they would not hesitate to shoot first and skip the questions entirely. Maddock had figured the odds of them getting shot out of the sky on approach were about even. That they had beaten those odds did not fill Maddock with confidence. They would have to get a lot closer on their next pass.

Bones' voice crackled in his ear again. "So, how are we gonna do this?"

Maddock considered his very short list of options as, below them, the Pope and his entourage stepped off the first escalator, and hastened along the dog-leg-crooked landing to the second escalator. Ribeiro and his hulking goon were close on their heels. Even from the high vantage, Maddock could see a glint of gold flashing from under Hugo's arm as he moved. Maddock reckoned that, in less than a minute, they would all be on the main landing and shortly thereafter, concealed from view for the duration of the elevator ride to the parking area.

"The cardinal's bodyguard has the reliquary. If we can get it away from him, we'll end this."

"I think my comms are fritzing," Bones said, his voice tinged with sarcasm. "Because it sounded like you just restated the problem."

"Noticed that, did you?" Maddock sighed. "Just follow my lead."

If Ribeiro convinced the Swiss Guard to let him accompany the Pope on the elevator—and Maddock did not doubt that he would be able to do so—it would provide him ample time and opportunity to carry out his deadly plan.

Which meant he and Bones had to get the reliquary away from Hugo before the party reached the elevator.

Maddock adjusted course slightly, lining up on the escalator like a jet pilot homing in on runway landing lights, and began flapping the wings—pumping the brakes up and down to reduce speed and, as a consequence, aerodynamic lift, which had the effect of turning the paraglider into a more-or-less conventional parachute. His momentum kept him moving in the desired direction, but the ground was coming up fast. He could see the escalator directly below, maybe fifty feet. The angle of the slope almost perfectly matched his own descent and the parallel moving stairways—one rising, one falling—created a vertiginous sensation of spinning counter-clockwise. He had to fight the impulse to correct course, and instead focused on the brutish figure that had just stepped from the escalator and onto the broad landing below.

Hugo was staring back at him, his piggish ogre face twisted in what was either a snarl of contempt or a smile of anticipation.

This is really going to suck, Maddock thought as the big man's free hand curled into a fist.

At the last instant before impact, Maddock bent his knees and pulled hard on the brakes, flaring the chute for landing. The stutter-step threw off Hugo's timing and instead of connecting solidly with Maddock's face—his presumed target—his punch instead glanced off

Maddock's booted feet. The blow spun Maddock around but he still had just enough forward momentum to slam into Hugo.

Under any other circumstances, the collision would have had about as much effect as a ping-pong ball striking an anvil, but Hugo's mistimed punch had shifted his center of gravity just enough that the bump sent him stumbling. He reflexively threw out his arms to regain his balance, and inadvertently flung the reliquary away. The heavy chest landed on the long red carpet with an ominous thud.

Maddock extended his legs, trying to reach the solid surface underneath him, but there was still enough air flowing under his glider wing to keep him from finding a purchase. As he twisted beneath the canopy, he saw the scene around him playing out like a panoramic shot in a movie. Hugo still stumbling across the landing... The reliquary, lying on its side atop the carpet runner... Ribeiro half-turning, his gaze focused on the golden chest, reaching out to it, shouting something... The grim-faced Swiss Guardsmen in their utilitarian black suits, hustling a barely visible white-robed figure under the canopy, toward the waiting elevators... One of them breaking from the pack in order to pull the cardinal along....

Then, Maddock was looking past the railing, over the tops of café umbrellas and beyond that, blue sky and the yawning emptiness below.

Still pawing for a foothold and flaring hard to avoid getting pulled back into the sky, he craned his head around to get another look.

Ribeiro was resisting the efforts of his would-be savior, gesturing frantically toward the abandoned reliquary.

The reliquary.

Maddock's gaze fixed on the golden chest. All he had to do was pick it up and chuck it over the side of the mountain, and the ordeal would all be over, but despite the fact that the reliquary was only a few steps away, it remained maddeningly out of reach.

He had to cut loose from the wing.

Letting go of the brake toggles, he groped for the quick-release carabiners that bound him to the paraglider, but before he could depress the locking button, Hugo blindsided him, sending him reeling across the landing. His boot soles scuffed uselessly across the concrete, the wind tugging at his canopy, dragging him toward the edge of the landing. As he staggered backward, he saw Hugo barreling toward him, fists raised and pumping the air like pistons. Just beyond him, the Swiss Guard who had been trying to help Ribeiro was striding toward the reliquary.

"No!" Maddock cried out. "It's—"

That was all he got out before one of Hugo's meaty fists slammed into him, hurling him against the safety rail. The double impact knocked the figurative wind from Maddock, but a gust of actual wind filled the ram air canopy above, snapping the cables taut and partially lifting him off his feet.

But Hugo had no intention of letting him escape back into the relative safety of the sky. As Maddock started to rise, the big man seized his harness straps and forced him back down, slamming him into the rail again.

Pain stabbed through Maddock's entire body. The bulky backpack and reserve chute had provided a little cushioning, but he could feel his ribs separating. Another hit like that, and his vertebrae would crack apart like walnuts. Desperate, he started swinging, throwing wild punches at Hugo's pig-like face, swatting his ears, but the big ogre shrugged off the blows, and then raised his helpless victim up in preparation for a final, decisive strike.

As he was lifted, Maddock caught a glimpse of the last Swiss Guard protector stepping into a waiting elevator car, a golden burden in his hands, and knew that it had all been for nothing. He had failed.

THIRTEEN

Cardinal Sergio Ribeiro's heart was racing, but this was only partly because of the frantic descent from the summit.

Maddock had nearly ruined everything.

He tried to draw a deep, calming breath, but only managed a hitched half-gasp. He tried again.

Better.

The elevator car vibrated gently as it descended. Beside him, his sworn enemy likewise labored to catch his breath, even as his protectors questioned him, checking for any injuries that might have been sustained in the mad dash to safety. Just beyond them, another of the bodyguards stood by the doors, holding the reliquary.

Ribeiro glanced down at his right hand, which still gripped the relic.

Maddock had nearly ruined everything, but *nearly* was not the same as *completely*. Ribeiro exhaled a prayer. "God be praised."

"Indeed, *Cardinale*," the Pope said, with a faint chuckle of relief. "That was… Exciting."

Ribeiro fought the urge to sneer, instead turning to the man who now carried the golden vessel. All he had to do was place the disc inside it, and the deed would be done. The burst of ionizing radiation would deliver slow but certain death upon them all.

The bodyguard shook his head gently. "Do not concern yourself, Eminence. I will carry it for you."

Ribeiro managed to hide his dismay behind a smile.

Be patient, he told himself. *An opportunity will present itself.*

The elevator car shuddered to a stop and the doors slid open. One of the Swiss Guard edged out, checking to make sure the path to the motorcade was clear, and then turned to the others and began barking orders in German. As it was the second-most common language in Brazil, Ribeiro understood well enough to know that the commanding officer had just ordered the man with the reliquary to accompany the cardinal in one of the trailing vehicles.

Ribeiro's heart stuttered again. "Wait," he gasped, fixing his stare on the Guard commander. He continued in halting German. "You saw the road. You know how difficult that way is. There are many places where these assassins could be waiting to attack. That may have been what the parachutists intended. To drive the Holy Father into an ambush."

Ribeiro could see that this assessment resonated with the other man. "Do you know another way, Eminence?"

"The train." Ribeiro gestured in the direction of the path leading down to the station. "It is a journey of only twenty minutes. And the assassins will not expect us to be traveling that way."

The commander's eyes darted from side to side, clearly contemplating the tactical advantages and disadvantages of the suggestion. Ribeiro sensed that his argument had failed to gain traction, and so instead appealed to a higher power. He shifted his gaze to the pontiff.

"Holiness, you must trust me. The train is the best way to get off this mountain."

The Pope stared back for a moment, and then his

eyes shifted to his protector. "Commander, what do you think?"

"He is correct about the road. But the train has no armor. If we are attacked while riding it, it will be difficult to defend."

"But they will not expect us to use the train," Ribeiro insisted.

The commander sighed. "Frankly, I doubt there will be an attack. The parachutists did not appear to be armed. I think their only intention was to disrupt this appearance."

The Pope nodded slowly. "I am inclined to agree with you." Then he smiled and faced Ribeiro again. "However, the cardinal seems to want very much to accompany me on a train ride. Perhaps it will give us an opportunity to resolve some of our differences."

Ribeiro bowed his head, hiding his smile. "I am certain it will, Holiness."

FOURTEEN

Bones snarled in impotent rage as, twenty feet below him, the cardinal's brutish bodyguard lifted Maddock into the air, preparing to slam him against the rail and break him in two. There was no easy way to shed altitude fast enough to be of assistance to Maddock. Flapping the wing would get him down, but it would still take a couple seconds, and by then, Maddock would already be broken in two.

There was however a hard way.

Bones' gripped the twin quick release carabiners on the front of his harness, flipped up the red safety cover with his thumbs, and then squeezed the release button. The mechanisms detached from the chute straps with an ominous snapping sound. The wing, suddenly relieved of its two hundred-odd pound burden, seemed to leap into the sky of its own accord, snatched away by the wind to sail unguided out over the forest. Bones just dropped straight down like an anchor.

Right onto the big goon's head.

Bones flexed his legs on contact, absorbing some of the energy from the impact, and then shifted his weight sideways and tucked his body into a roll, just as he'd learned on the first day of Airborne jump school. Unfortunately, that technique had been designed with ground landings in mind. The collision with Maddock's assailant had taken place at head level for the man, a good six feet off the ground. Bones realized this too late to do anything about it, and a half-second later, slammed down hard onto the concrete landing. His helmet probably saved his life, keeping his skull from breaking open like a cantaloupe against the hard surface, but he still saw stars sizzling in front of his eyes. The breath was driven from his lungs in a single forceful exhalation, leaving him open-mouthed like a beached fish, unable even to gasp. For a second or two, he felt numb, but as the shock wore off, the pain slammed through him like a freight train. Yet, through it all, he could see the hulking bodyguard reeling from the blow, clutching his head with both hands. As the man staggered away, Bones could also see Maddock leaning against the rail, held upright by the still-inflated paraglider canopy hovering above, and still very much alive.

Well, at least that part went according to plan, Bones thought.

Maddock was looking around, searching the landing, but Bones knew he wouldn't find what he sought. The Pope's security detail had already departed, taking along Cardinal Ribeiro and the reliquary. There was a very good chance that the Cardinal had already used his nuclear option, in which case the battle was already lost, until they knew for certain, they had to keep trying, and that meant continuing the pursuit. Bones managed to raise one hand, pointing toward the elevators, but was unable to find the breath to speak.

Maddock seemed to understand, nevertheless. With a pained grimace, he pushed away from the rail and grasped the brake toggles, retaking control of his chute.

There wasn't enough wind for him to simply jump back into the sky; to launch, he would need the added lift of air pushing against the canopy. He would need a running start, and while there was more than enough room on the landing for him to manage that, there was one big obstacle in his way.

A few steps away from them both, Ribeiro's ogre was shaking off the effects of the drop-in attack. Blood was streaming down from the top of his head, where one of Bones' boots had peeled away a section of scalp the size of a beer coaster, but the wound seemed to only enrage him. He wiped the blood from his eyes, flicking it away with a disdainful shake of his hand, and then started toward Maddock.

Bones heaved himself up onto hands and knees, curling his toes under and pushing up into a four-point stance, like a defensive tackle poised at the scrimmage line, waiting for the snap. His breath returned with a pained gasp. "No, you don't," he growled, and then exploded forward.

The bodyguard's eyes flashed toward him, his weight shifting to meet Bones' rush. The man was about the same height as Bones, but a good fifty pounds heavier, most of it muscle. Even before his SEAL training, Bones had learned a thing or two about hand-to-hand fighting, but because of his size, he rarely had occasion to train against someone even bigger than himself. He had a fleeting premonition of splattering against the immovable bulk like a bug on a windshield. The collision wasn't quite as bad as that, but it did stop Bones dead in his tracks without budging the big man an inch. Bones wrapped his arms around the man's considerable girth and tried to pivot into a throw, but his foe remained immovable.

But as futile as his attempt was, Bones had accomplished his sole objective. From his clinch, he could see Maddock running across the landing. The lines connecting him to the paraglider snapped taut with the additional rush of air, and then just as he was about to hit the rail on the opposite side of the landing, he lifted his legs and was flying again.

Mission accomplished, Bones thought. He relaxed his hold on the bodyguard and tried to push away, but before he could, his foe's arms curled around him in a bear hug. The man shifted his weight, and Bones, realizing that he was the one about to be thrown, reversed again, dropping lower and wrapping his arms around the man's left leg just as the latter began his attack.

Bones felt his feet leaving the ground and whipped his body in the direction of the intended throw, adding his momentum to unbalance his foe. The big man spun out of control, but he did not let go of Bones. After a few staggering steps, he crashed into the railing and then toppled over it, taking Bones along with him.

The fall was short and the subsequent landing, painful. A few feet below the level of the landing was a fixed stairway, which only a few moments before, had been crowded with people who had come to the mountain expecting a very different spectacle. The throng broke apart, visitors screaming and fighting to get out of the way of the two combatants.

Bones could feel the other man's hands on him, trying to pry him loose, and so held on even tighter. His feet pedaled the air, and then, miraculously, made contact with something solid. He braced himself against it and pushed, sending them both tumbling down the stairs.

The next few seconds were a blur of pain and motion. Bones' helmet and backpack blunted some of the punishment, but every somersault put him between the hard anvil of the concrete steps and the prodigiously heavy hammer of his foe's bulk, and as they careered down the stairs, gaining momentum, the hits came harder and faster.

With a sudden lurch, they were free-falling, but only for a fleeting instant before crashing down again. A muted crack accompanied the abrupt landing, and as the downward plunge continued, the noise repeated with machine-gun ferocity. It was not the sound of Bones' actual bones splintering apart, but tree branches and woody shrubs, crushed under the rolling bodies. The green blur all around him confirmed Bones' suspicion that they had careened off the stairs and onto the surrounding hillside.

The soft earth was considerably more forgiving than the cement stairs, but the realization of where he was— where he was headed—sent a cold spike of fear through him. He'd gotten a very good look at the area from the sky above. Corcovado reminded him of an enormous granite shark fin, jutting up from the forest floor—to the west, it sloped down at a steep angle, but in every other direction, the ruff of foliage at the crest ended at the edge of a sheer cliff. Bones didn't have to consult a compass to know that he was hurtling toward a precipice.

He let go of his foe and tried to push away. Bones didn't know if the man was still hanging onto him, or if he was even still alive, but the relentless tumble was holding them together like Velcro. Frantic, he simply flung his arms out, spread-eagling trying to find something to hold onto, or at the very least, use his body as a friction brake.

His left arm hooked on something—a low hanging tree branch. He managed to curl his hand around it, but the brittle wood snapped in two, unable to hold weight of two men. Yet, in the brief instant before the limb broke, he felt the other man's clutch loosening perceptibly. And the broken branch was still in his hand.

He stabbed the stick down into the ground, dragging it through the soil. His descent slowed, and then slowed further still as the cardinal's ogre peeled away and kept going. Bones pushed harder on the stick, willing it to dig down and pierce the granite underneath. Above him, a long furrow marked the path of his descent. Below....

He looked down, and then immediately regretted it.

"Holy crap!" he gasped.

There was nothing there. No more trees. No more ground. Just empty space, into which his foe had already vanished.

It took him a moment to realize that he had stopped moving. His feet were dangling over the edge but the rest of him was on solid ground and not going anywhere. He lay there on the slope for a few more seconds, afraid to move, afraid even to breathe a sigh of relief.

That was too close, he thought.

A fluttering noise above distracted him. It was Maddock, soaring overhead, his paraglider snapping and popping in the wind as he climbed back into the sky.

"Your turn," he muttered, and then sagged against the hillside, wondering how the hell he was going to get back up the slope.

FIFTEEN

Even though he cleared the rail of the landing, Maddock's wing didn't have enough lift to bear him aloft, so for a few seconds, he lost altitude. Fortunately, the hillside below was sloping away at an even faster rate, giving him plenty of room to build up the forward velocity needed to achieve aerodynamic lift. He pushed the speedbar to its maximum, which pulled the leading edge of the canopy down, creating the airfoil shape of an airplane wing, and after a few seconds of gliding descent, he began to climb again.

A gentle tug on the left brake brought him back around in a slow turn. The mountain loomed directly ahead but as he straightened out to resume climbing, he judged that he had enough altitude to avoid crashing into it, as long as he stayed to the right of the actual summit and the towering statue that rose an additional hundred feet above it.

He found the landing and the glass-enclosed elevator shaft where Bones and Hugo were locked in a titanic struggle. That Bones had not already put the ogre in a submission hold was cause for concern; had Bones met his match? Maddock felt a pang of guilt for leaving his partner to fight the battle alone, but knew that if he didn't stop Ribeiro, Bones' fate would be of little consequence.

He didn't allow himself to consider the possibility that he was already too late.

He steered to the right, spotting the parking area where the papal motorcade was lined up and ready for a hasty exit. He was a little surprised that they weren't already underway. As he sailed over the parking lot, he attracted the attention of the police officers waiting with their motorcycles, but saw no sign at all of the Pope and his Swiss Guard protectors.

Where are they?

He banked again, coming around for another pass, but still saw no activity at all in the parking area. Were they still in the elevator car?

That didn't seem possible. It had been at least a minute or two, maybe even more, since his launch. No elevator was that slow.

What am I missing?

Had the Pope's protectors decided to shelter in place? Were there secret tunnels under the mountain?

Amalia's voice echoed in his head. *There are only three ways to get to the top of Monte Cristo.*

Three ways up, three ways down.

He doubted the Swiss Guard were planning to take the Pope trekking through the rainforest, and since they clearly weren't using the road, that left only the train.

He searched the hillside below until he found the railway depot at the end of the line. The path leading from the elevators to the station was partly obscured by the overhanging foliage, but through the covering, he could just make out the railway itself, a narrow ribbon of cleared ground, with parallel rails running down the center, and evenly spaced poles supporting power lines along one side. As his gaze followed the descending rails, he spotted a boxy red shape trundling down the tracks.

The train had just left the station.

He was a little surprised that the Swiss Guard would have chosen to utilize the tram for their escape. It was a poor choice, tactically speaking, especially when the alternative was a convoy of up-armored SUVs with a police escort.

But it was perfect for what Cardinal Ribeiro had planned.

Maddock knew he had to get aboard the train and knew exactly what that would require of him. He veered toward it, pushing the speedbar to the max again as he lined up on the trackway some fifty feet below.

The train was about a hundred yards further along, but he was rapidly closing the distance. It consisted of two linked light-rail tram cars. From his overhead vantage, Maddock could see a metal structure rising from the top of one car to make contact with the nearly invisible electrical lines suspended high above the tracks. The train did not appear to be moving very fast. Ten miles per hour, give or take, which was considerably slower than Maddock's current forward velocity. He eased off the speed bar and went to about fifty percent brakes, but was still about to overtake the train.

He flapped the wing, shedding both speed and altitude. The top of the train was just thirty feet below... Twenty... Fifteen... The high-voltage lines were easy to distinguish now, the cross-members supporting them flashing past at regular four-second intervals.

He added more brake until he was matching the train's speed, right above the trailing car. Too slow to sustain lift, he was losing altitude rapidly, but he kept his focus on the crosspieces of the power lines, synchronizing himself to their rhythm.

One... Two... Three... Four... One... Two... Three....

PULL!

He popped the quick-release, cutting away the paraglider, and dropped straight down, arms and legs tucked in to avoid the lethal power lines snaking by to either side. As soon as he felt the metal surface under his boots, he threw his body forward, flattening out atop the car a fraction of a second before another crosspiece passed just inches above him.

Maddock wasted no time sidling over to the edge of the roof. The thump of his landing would have reverberated through the car like a drumbeat, alerting the Swiss Guard—and Ribeiro—to the presence of a hitchhiker. The former would be waiting for him with guns drawn. The latter might do something even worse.

A peek revealed folding doors positioned near the rear of the car, and something else that gave Maddock a faint ray of hope. The rear car of the train was empty. The Pope and his party had boarded the forward car, which meant his arrival had probably gone unnoticed.

This revelation did not lessen his sense of urgency. The cardinal wasn't going to wait until the train reached the end of the line to strike. Indeed, it might already be too late, though Maddock refused to entertain that dire possibility.

He leaned out again, getting a mental snapshot of the car's layout. There were two doors—one fore, one aft. At each end was a small control booth, similarly unoccupied since the train was being controlled, presumably, from the front of the lead car. The passenger area in between consisted of row upon row of molded plastic seats, with a single narrow aisle running down the middle. There was no door or bridge connecting the cars, which left him only one way of getting to the front of the train.

He low crawled forward, traversing the length of the car in a matter of seconds. The gap between the cars was only about two feet. The train's slow speed made for a gentle ride, but as he looked across to the opposite roof, Maddock saw the track bed flashing by and felt a faint sense of vertigo. He looked away quickly, fixing his gaze on the roof of the lead car, and reached out to pull himself across.

Despite the need for speed, he moved slowly, taking care not to announce his presence with a lot of noise. When he was sure of his hold on the roof of the lead car, he edged over the side once again for a peek, and then drew back hastily as he spotted a man in a black suit stationed at the rear door, facing out.

Guess this is the one, he thought.

He didn't think the man had noticed him, but now that he knew he had the right car, there was nothing to be gained by delaying the inevitable. Gripping the edge of the roof, he swung out over the side, and whipped back toward the doors, hitting them solidly with both booted feet.

The folding panels exploded inward, ripped off their hinges, and flattened the hapless Swiss Guard stationed there. Maddock let go, dropping into a crouch atop the broken pieces. The arc of his swing left him precariously unbalanced, but he caught himself on his elbows, and then sprang back to his feet.

The dynamic entry had caught everyone else in the train completely by surprise, but in the moment it took for him to rise, all eyes turned toward him.

The Swiss Guard reacted almost instantaneously, drawing matte-black semi-automatic pistols as they stepped into the center aisle, intent on taking down this intruder even as they shielded the Pope with their own bodies. Beyond them, near the front of the car, the Pope and Cardinal Ribeiro had jumped to their feet, turning to look at the disturbance. One Swiss Guard stood beside them, the golden reliquary held before him.

Maddock threw his hands up quickly to demonstrate that he posed no threat, but before he could utter a syllable of explanation, he saw the cardinal's eyes flash from recognition to anger to resolve.

Ribeiro turned toward the man holding the reliquary and reached out to it. His movements were unhurried; he seemed almost to be moving in slow motion.

"Stop him!" Maddock shouted, pointing one still upraised hand at the cardinal. He knew that exhortation wouldn't be enough to get the Swiss Guard on his side, so he added, "Radioactive!"

The Swiss Guard responded as if the word itself was potentially lethal, recoiling in horror, but then they seemed to understand what he was trying to communicate to them, following his pointing finger to look at Ribeiro.

The cardinal, aware that he was now the focus of attention, took an abrupt step forward, closing on the man with the reliquary, and gave the chest a hard shove. Despite his advanced years, the suddenness of the cardinal's attack caught the younger bodyguard unprepared, and the considerable weight of the gold-covered stone artifact did the rest. The cardinal's thrust slammed the reliquary into the other man's solar plexus, driving him back against the forward door where he slumped, stunned, the chest still clutched in his hands. Ribeiro dropped to his knees, reaching for the reliquary again, and this time, Maddock could see a silvery disc of metal in the cardinal's outstretched hand.

The Swiss Guard seemed to grasp that Ribeiro was about to do something terrible to the man that they were sworn to protect, and so reacted by removing the Pope from the immediate area. Two of them grabbed the pontiff, thrusting him down the center aisle toward Maddock, while the others closed on the cardinal, shouting for him to desist.

As the Pope fell into his arms, Maddock lost sight of Ribeiro, but he knew that if the cardinal succeeded in putting the radioactive relic into the neutron-reflective container, triggering a criticality event, survivability would be a function of time and distance. Sixty years ago, a brief exposure to the Demon Core had been enough to cause malignant mutations in the bone marrow of a man sitting twelve feet away. Maddock had no idea how much neutron and gamma radiation would be released if criticality lasted even a few seconds longer, or what the minimum safe distance was, but the tram car was definitely feeling a lot smaller.

We need to get off this train.

As if to underscore this thought, he heard one of the Swiss Guard shouting. It sounded like German, but Maddock didn't need a translation.

Save the Holy Father.

Maddock wrapped one arm around the older man and half-dragged, half-carried him to the rear exit. Through the open doorway, he could see the gravel track bed rolling by, and just beyond it, a craggy wall of moss-covered granite. Even though the train was only moving at a sedate ten miles per hour, hitting the ground—or worse, the wall beyond—at that speed, was going to hurt. It would be even rougher on the octogenarian Pope, but hurt was better than dead, and Maddock had a crazy idea that—if it worked—might soften the landing a little.

He pivoted, putting his back to the doorway, and shouted, "Hang on!"

Then, he jumped.

As they fell backward, Maddock pulled the ripcord for his reserve parachute. There was a slight shudder as the spring-loaded launch mechanism propelled the chute straight up into the air.

It required about three seconds of free fall for a deployed parachute to inflate and begin creating the necessary resistance to slow the rate of descent—a bare minimum of one hundred vertical feet. Even with the addition of the train's forward velocity, the four feet separating the deck of the car from the track bed was not even enough to allow the chute to unfurl, much less begin filling with air, but air wasn't what Maddock had been hoping to catch.

He barely had time to close his free hand around the other man before an abrupt jolt yanked his harness tight around his body. Above, the canopy and several feet of parachute cord had snagged on the cross member of a power pole, wrapping around it like a grappling hook.

They were still in motion, but instead of falling, the two men were now swinging at the end of the parachute lines in a rising arc that was just slightly askew from parallel to the tracks. The train pulled away, slowly at first, then seeming to accelerate as their forward momentum was exhausted, and they began to swing back in the other direction.

Maddock felt a moment of apprehension as the rebound trajectory took them back toward the train, but it was now moving a lot faster than they were. The corner of the rear car passed by a full half-second before the pendulum motion swung them over the tracks.

The arc shortened and then reversed again, swinging gently away. Maddock, surprised that his desperate gamble had actually paid off, just sagged in relief, making no effort to arrest their motion.

Fifty yards away, a brilliant flash of electric blue—like an arc welder—shone out from the windows of the lead tram car, then blinked out just as quickly.

Still clinging to Maddock's chest, the Pope gasped, "What was that?"

Maddock shook his head sadly. "Nothing holy."

EPILOGUE

A rousing cheer greeted Matt Barnaby as he stepped over the transom to board *Sea Foam*. Maddock—who had accompanied his crewmate from the hospital, where he had spent the last two days receiving treatment for, among other things, a broken collarbone—hung back, letting Matt have the spotlight for a moment.

As the clapping subsided, Bones pointed to the sling holding Matt's left arm immobile against his chest. "I'm guessing you had a close encounter with one of those naked dudes in Carnaval?"

"Don't hate me just because I've got painkillers," Matt shot back.

Bones uttered a dismissive snort. "Got my own prescription."

In fact, both he and Maddock had received medical treatment following the previous day's events at the summit of Corcovado, but their injuries—while painful—had not been serious enough to warrant an overnight stay.

The doctors had also been able to confirm that Maddock had not received a dose of ionizing radiation during the brief criticality event. The Swiss Guard and the train operator had not been so lucky, but it was hoped that immediate full-spectrum treatment would prevent, or at least mitigate, the onset of acute radiation syndrome.

Before he could step over onto the boat, a heavily-accented female voice called out from behind him. "Did we miss the celebration?"

Maddock turned to see two women, both wearing bikinis, strolling down the dock, carrying a large Styrofoam cooler between them. Scantily clad women were hardly an uncommon sight at the marina where *Sea Foam* was moored, but Maddock nevertheless did a double-take when he recognized the new arrivals: Amalia and Ana.

"Are you freaking kidding?" Bones chortled after an appreciative whistle. "I think it just started."

"This who you guys have been hanging out with?" hooted a grinning Willis.

"About time you let the rest of us in on the fun," added Corey, who was staring, goggle-eyed at the women.

"Oh, right," Matt grumbled. "Because we've been partying non-stop."

Willis grinned. "From what Bones has told us, sure sounds that way."

The two women set the cooler on the dock, and then unselfconsciously embraced Maddock.

"What are you doing here?" Maddock asked Amalia as they hugged. He had spoken to her over the phone the previous day, but the call had been brief. She had her hands full managing the fallout—figuratively speaking—from what had happened on the mountaintop. Even though they had thwarted an assassination plot against the Pope, there were still a lot of legal hurdles to clear.

"I promised to show you Carnaval," she said. "There are still two days left."

Maddock winced at the thought of doing anything more physically demanding than reclining in a chaise lounge on the foredeck. "Thanks, but I think I have to agree with Matt. I'm a little partied out."

"I thought you might feel that way, so I brought the party to you." She bent over the cooler, lifting the lid to reveal a couple dozen brown glass bottles nestled in ice chips.

"Okay, I think I can handle that," Maddock said. He glanced back at his crewmen who were still staring at the women as if hypnotized, and shook his head sadly. "I guess chivalry is dead."

Willis and Corey nearly tripped over each other in their haste to retrieve the cooler. That Bones did not beat them to the punch was testimony to the extent of his injuries. Although he had not sustained any fractures, his body was one enormous bruise. He did however reach out a hand to help Ana come aboard.

"I also wanted to give you the good news," Amalia went on, a little more reserved. "You've been cleared of all criminal charges."

"Cleared?" Bones scoffed. "They should be giving us friggin' medals."

"Don't be too greedy," Amalia cautioned. "The police commissioner was very angry that we didn't simply warn them about what the cardinal was planning."

"Like they would have believed us," said Maddock.

"We'll never know," Amalia replied with a shrug. "Regardless, they can't very well arrest the men who saved the Holy Father. And *he* is very grateful."

"Maybe he could make us honorary Swiss Guards," said Bones. "Or better yet, Templar Knights."

Maddock shot a glance at him. "Templars? You're kidding, right?"

Bones shrugged. "I don't know. I just remembered the way the Swiss Guards dress and thought, no freaking way."

Maddock shook his head, then took Amalia's hand and escorted her onto the boat. "What about Ribeiro?"

Amalia hesitated before answering. "He will not be charged either."

"What? You're kidding?"

"It would be very embarrassing for the Church if it was known that a cardinal plotted against the Holy Father."

"But they could get him on other stuff. He killed Sam Decker."

"He would not live to see a prison cell. He is very sick with radiation poisoning. He probably will not last the week."

"I thought with the new treatments—"

Amalia shook her head. "His sickness was already advanced when he was brought to hospital. He tested the relic the night before he made his attempt on the Holy Father, and received a lethal dose of radiation."

"He should have worn that mask," Bones remarked.

"He did. And he wore a lead apron to protect himself. It wasn't enough."

Maddock nodded in understanding. "Lead can shield from gamma rays, but not neutron radiation."

"So how did the indigenous shamans avoid getting dosed?"

"I don't know. Maybe they didn't. Or maybe it has something to do with the reliquary."

Amalia went on. "The Church and the government are in agreement that no one must know what happened. Not any of it. It's bad enough that a cardinal tried to assassinate the Holy Father, but with a nuclear device?" She shook her head. "I promised them you would keep the secret. You will, won't you?"

"Mum's the word." Bones mimed zipping his lips and turning the key on an invisible padlock, which he then slipped into the waistband of his shorts, right above his fly, while wiggling his hips suggestively.

"You will have to sign legally binding non-disclosure agreements," she added, a little hesitantly. "Before you leave the country, that is."

Maddock gave her a sidelong glance. "So, no hurry, then?"

"You are not leaving?"

"We came down here to do a job, and it's not finished. Unless… You aren't firing us, are you?"

Her eyes widened as if horrified by the thought. "Of course not. I just… I did not think you would want to stay here after everything."

"I'd hate for somebody else to find those Roman artifacts."

She flashed him a cautious smile. "You know, they may not even exist."

Maddock laughed. "Then I guess we could be here a while."

The End

If you enjoyed *Destination-Rio,* try *Destination-Luxor,* book two of *the Destination-Adventure* series!

From the author of OUTPOST and EXILE

SEAN ELLIS

DESTINATION:
LUXOR

A DANE MADDOCK DESTINATION ADVENTURE

Enjoy this preview of

DESTINATION: LUXOR
A Dane Maddock Adventure

"Are you sure we're in the right country?"

Dane Maddock glanced over at his friend and partner, Uriah "Bones" Bonebrake, and braced himself for another awful joke. "Why do you ask?"

"We've been here two days and I haven't seen anyone walking like this." Without breaking stride, Bones turned and struck an odd pose—wrists, elbows and knees bent at sharp angles, his left hand bobbing sinuously in front of his face like a cobra about to strike, his right held at the small of his back like a duck's tail. The effect was somewhat blunted by the large beige and black Pelican BA-22 carry-on case he gripped in his right hand, and the even larger hockey gear bag slung over one shoulder, but that didn't stop him from adopting a falsetto voice and vocalizing what Maddock assumed was meant to be the harmony from a Bangles' song. "Way-oh-way-ohhh-way-ohohohh. Walk like an Egyptian."

His antics earned a few curious glances from passersby, but the faces just as quickly looked away, clearly intimidated by his appearance. At six feet-five inches, Bones towered above everyone, including the almost six-foot-tall Maddock, but the height disparity was only part of it. Bones' Native American heritage gave him a dark complexion, not unlike the skin-tone of the Egyptians around them, but his long pony tail and complete lack of facial hair distinctly set him apart as something else entirely.

Maddock regarded his friend for a few seconds and

then, in his best approximation of a Jeopardy contestant, said, "Who is Steve Martin?"

Bones frowned. "Steve Martin?" He shook his head. "Dude, I worry about you sometimes."

"If you don't know who Steve Martin is, maybe I should be worried about you."

"I know who Steve Martin is," Bones shot back, sourly. "I just don't see what he has to do with this."

"You're kidding, right? King Tut?" Maddock, fully aware that it was completely out of character for him, nevertheless adopted a pose similar to what Bones had displayed, and sing-songed, "'How'd you get so funk-y? Did you do the mon-key?'"

Bones just blinked at him.

Maddock resumed walking down the train platform, passing ornate columns—replicas of the actual historic artifacts that were ubiquitous throughout the region—interspersed with vending machines. "I would have thought you, of all people, would get that reference."

Bones snorted. "Keep singing. Even if I don't figure it out, at least it will scare the locals off."

As if on cue, a young Egyptian man, bolder than the others, stepped in front of them. "Taxi? You need taxi?"

Despite his impulse to politely dismiss the man, Maddock simply ignored him. Showing even a little deference would only encourage more offers, or so all the guidebooks said, and since most of the supplicants were actually con artists hoping to bilk unwary tourists with bait-and-switch games, there was no reason to feel bad about being a little rude.

The Egyptian repeated the offer a couple more times, then fell back, setting his sights on someone else disembarking from the overnight express train, but another entrepreneur quickly took his place. Unlike the first Egyptian, who had been wearing Western attire, this man wore a more traditional jellabiya long garment of light blue cotton, and a white turban.

"Camel ride? You want camel ride? Just seventy-five pounds. Valley of the Kings? Deir el-Bahari? My cousin take you there."

They actually were headed for the first location, the famed archaeological site, where in 1922, archaeologist Howard Carter had discovered the treasure-laden tomb of Pharaoh Tutankhamun, but despite the fact that seventy-five Egyptian pounds converted to about five American dollars, Maddock was wary of both the offer and the suggested mode of transportation.

Bones either shared his antipathy or couldn't resist the opening for an off-color joke. "I'm not getting my moose knuckle anywhere near a camel toe."

Maddock sighed and dead-panned. "Didn't see that coming."

"You know," Bones went on, conversationally, as they continued down the platform, leaving the camel-tour vendor behind, "When you said we had a job in Luxor, this wasn't exactly what came to mind?"

Maddock had heard variations on this theme several times during the flight to Cairo and the subsequent overnight train ride along the Nile River. Bones had been crestfallen to learn that they were headed to Egypt instead of to the Luxor Casino on the Las Vegas Strip."

"We're treasure hunters, Bones. People don't find treasure in Vegas. They lose it. I'm saving you from a lot of heartache and disappointment. Besides. I would have thought you'd be sick of casinos by now." Bones' uncle, Crazy Charlie, operated a casino on the Cherokee reservation in North Carolina. Bones had even briefly worked there as a bouncer after leaving the military.

Bones wrinkled his nose distastefully. "Next time you get the urge to save me from anything... Don't. And if you think there's any treasure left to be found here, you're fooling yourself. This place was picked clean thousands of years ago. Now it's just another tourist trap in the desert, only with more flies and dysentery."

Although it was hard to argue with any of what Bones had just said, Maddock knew that there were still serious archaeological discoveries being made in the desert surrounding Luxor. It was just such a discovery that had brought the two of them here.

Maddock might have called them "treasure hunters" but he was motivated more by his passion for history and exploration, not to mention a craving for adventure, than by mere lust for gold. While he needed to make a living like anyone, it was the looking not the finding that satisfied the yearning in his soul, and he knew that Bones, despite his rough edges, felt the same way, which was why their partnership had flourished, despite getting off to a rocky start.

They had met in the Navy, during the first phase of SEAL training. Maddock, had been an uptight young officer looking to advance his career, and Bones had been a hard-drinking, hard-partying enlisted seaman with a chip on his shoulder as big as the Cherokee Nation. Against all odds, the two men had become friends, and then after leaving the service, had gone into business together as marine salvage and recovery experts. In the years that had followed, the two men had made astonishing discoveries in every far-flung corner of the globe, and saved the world once or twice along the way. Recently, they had started doing contract work for the Global Heritage Commission, a small agency working under the auspices of the United Nations, dedicated to protecting World Heritage sites. Most of their jobs involved underwater surveys, helping marine archaeologists document wrecks and submerged ruins. There was very little treasure involved, and even less glory, but it was satisfying work and it kept the lights on. Even more important to Maddock, it was an excuse to spend time underwater.

This particular job, which had brought them to the Egyptian desert, would probably not afford him a chance to get wet. An Egyptian archaeologist named Dr. Majdy, working in the Valley of the Kings on the west bank of the Nile River, had discovered an unfinished royal tomb containing what had initially appeared to be a deep cistern, still partially filled with water. Subsequent tests however indicated that the water in the cistern was fresh, and chemically identical to that found in the Nile River, nearly three miles away. Since it was not being replenished by rainwater, or any other external source, the only logical assumption was that it was not a cistern, but rather a well, probably fed by an uncharted subterranean tributary of the Nile. A dye test would likely confirm the existence of a passage connecting the well to the river, but Majdy wanted to conduct a survey to see if it might be part of an ancient water supply system, connecting to other undiscovered chambers, and to that end had contacted the Global Heritage Commission for technical assistance in conducting an underwater survey, which was how Maddock and Bones had gotten involved.

The actual survey would be done using a small

ROV—remotely-operated-vehicle—which Bones carried in the Pelican case. Not quite a meter long, and no bigger around than a gallon milk jug, the ROV—nicknamed Uma—could go places a person couldn't, which was advantageous since the water level in the cistern was more than a hundred feet down, and there was no telling what lay below the surface. Even if subterranean passages did lead back to the river, it was extremely unlikely that the channels would be large enough to accommodate a diver, but just in case, they had also brought along SCUBA gear.

They were hit up several more times as they made their way off the platform to pass through the station. There were offers of taxi service, camel safaris, and hot air balloon tours. One young man slyly inquired if they were interested in purchasing "authentic" ancient Egyptian artifacts. Maddock had to maintain a fierce grip on the strap of his gear bag to prevent some of the men from simply grabbing it off his shoulder. He didn't know if their intent was merely to bear his luggage to his taxi or hotel and then extort a large gratuity from him, or to simply abscond with it. It seemed prudent to leave that particular mystery unsolved.

The train station was decorated to resemble an ancient Egyptian temple, with white alabaster columns and false balconies inside, and an exterior sandstone beige façade adorned with an enormous stylized Egyptian vulture with outstretched golden wings above the entrance. A short flight of steps led down to the pavement where a line of taxis were waiting to bear the arriving passengers to their next destination. Maddock paused on the steps, letting the herd thin out a bit as he got his first good look at the city of Luxor.

First occupied more than five thousand years before the present, the city had been known to the ancient Egyptians as Wo'se—City of the Sceptre, signifying its status as the administrative center of Upper Egypt—and later as Niwt-'Imn—City of Amun, the chief deity of southern Egypt. Situated on the banks of the Nile River, about four hundred miles upriver from Cairo—or Memphis, as it was known in ancient times—the city had for a time, served as the capital of the unified Egyptian Kingdom. Many of the best-known names in ancient Egyptian history had lived, died and been buried there. The Greeks called it Thebes of the Hundred Gates, but by the time of Alexander the Great, the city's importance had already begun to wane, and by the First Century, it had become little more than a memory. The rediscovery of the ancient ruins by Napoleon's savants—scientific scholars who accompanied his invasion force in 1798—had not only resulted in the creation of the new science of Egyptology, but had also brought renewed interest in the Arab settlement known as al-'Uqṣur—the Palaces—later simplified to Luxor. Cairo had the pyramids and the Sphinx, but the real treasures of ancient Egypt were hidden in the sands outside Luxor, and despite more than two centuries of archaeological exploration—and five millennia of looting by tomb robbers, not all of them had been uncovered.

Modern Luxor looked to Maddock like an eclectic hodge-podge of weathered old Colonial-era architecture and newer utilitarian structures of brick and concrete. To his left, he could see the minaret of a mosque reaching up like an exclamation point from behind another building, while a few hundred yards in the opposite direction rose the white dome and bell towers of a Coptic Orthodox Church. The one-way two-lane street fronting the railway station was shared by cars and buses, as well as old motorcycles, donkey carts and even ornate horse-drawn four-wheeled carriages—called caleches. The air was hot and dry, despite the close proximity of the river, but while there were no clouds in the azure sky, there were strange bulbous shapes visible in the west, just above the horizon—hot air balloons, drifting on the wind.

He was still gazing up at them when he heard Bones calling to him. "Dude, I think that's our ride."

Maddock returned his attention to the pick-up lane and saw that an older-model red Peugeot sedan had slipped into the queue of blue-and-white liveried cabs. The passenger side window had been lowered and the driver was leaning across to wave a hand at them. They had been told to expect a car, but there was no way of knowing if this was actually it, or just one more local entrepreneur looking to score some tourist cash.

"I hope you're right," Maddock replied, starting forward.

As he drew closer, he was surprised to see that the driver was a woman. She appeared to be young—late twenties, perhaps—with olive complexion and fine features, but that was about all he could tell about her. The rest of her head was covered by a black hijab scarf.

A woman?

The revelation stopped him in his tracks.

He had seen quite a few women since arriving in Egypt the previous day, but had not actually interacted with any of them. Everybody he had dealt with—from the customs officials at the airport to the endless stream of touts at the station—had been male. The distribution of the sexes among his fellow travelers—both Egyptian and non-Egyptian—had been pretty even, so the disparity hadn't really registered with him

Although predominately Muslim, Egypt was not as strict about enforcing gender segregation as some neighboring countries, at least where visitors were concerned, but it was a different story for the locals, particularly in Upper Egypt, far from the more relaxed atmosphere of metropolitan centers like Cairo and Alexandria. Despite some progressive reforms during the Twentieth Century, the more recent rise in religious fundamentalism coupled with a flagging economy, had severely limited opportunities for women in a country that had once been ruled by the likes of Nefertiti and Cleopatra. The situation for Egyptian women was, by some accounts, the worst in the Arab world, with the highest rates of sexual harassment, honor killings and female genital mutilation.

Maddock knew from experience that interacting with a local female under such conditions might very well make her the subject of such abuse. Maybe a case of mistaken identity?

The woman locked eyes with him. Hers were almond-shaped and a deep chocolate brown. Then she smiled. No lipstick, but her teeth were dazzling. "Mr. Maddox?"

So much for that idea. "Uh... It's Maddock, actually," he said, stressing the last syllable.

She blinked, her sculpted eyebrows coming together in a look of confusion. "What's the difference?"

Maddock glanced around, checking to see if the exchange had attracted any undue attention, and discovered that at least one person had taken an interest.

"Here's how I remember it," Bones said, leaning down to get a better look at her. "Daffy is one mad duck. Singular. Donald and Daffy together would be mad ducks. Plural." He jerked a thumb in Maddock's direction. "He's just daffy."

Bones had clearly put a lot of thought into this explanation.

The woman blinked again, but her smile broadened, revealing dimples in her cheeks. "So just 'mad duck,'" she said. Her English was impeccable, with just a hint of a British accent. "I'll try to remember that."

"I wouldn't worry too much about it," Bones went on. "He's so desperate, he'll answer to anything. I'm Bones, but you can call me anytime."

"You are a very strange man, Anytime."

Maddock felt a mild surge of panic at his friend's typically forward behavior. What might get him a slap or a drink thrown in his face anywhere else could get him— or the woman—in serious trouble here. He stepped forward, intent on putting himself between Bones and the woman, but a flash of movement from the rear end of the car distracted him. As he turned to look, he saw a group of Egyptian men—a dozen, maybe more—closing with them, the nearest just a few steps away. All wore jellabiyas with turbans wrapped around heads and necks, but unlike the touts and scam artists who had been assailing them from the moment they stepped off the train, these men were strangely silent.

Maddock felt a tingle of apprehension. "Bones, I think—"

Before he could complete the thought, one of the men shouted something, and then, as if possessed of a single consciousness, they all charged.

ABOUT THE AUTHORS

David Wood is the USA Today bestselling author of the action-adventure series, The Dane Maddock Adventures, and many other works. He also writes fantasy under his David Debord pen name. When not writing, he hosts the Wood on Words podcast. David and his family live in Santa Fe, New Mexico. Visit him online at davidwoodweb.com.

Sean Ellis has authored and co-authored more than two dozen action-adventure novels, including the Nick Kismet adventures, the Jack Sigler/Chess Team series with Jeremy Robinson, and the Jade Ihara adventures with David Wood. He served with the Army National Guard in Afghanistan, and has a Bachelor of Science degree in Natural Resources Policy from Oregon State University. Sean is also a member of the International Thriller Writers organization. He currently resides in Arizona, where he divides his time between writing, adventure sports, and trying to figure out how to save the world. Learn more about Sean at seanellisauthor.com

50948421R00099

Made in the USA
Middletown, DE
28 June 2019